PIECE OF GRACE

A WILLOW GRACE FBI THRILLER

C.C. WEST

WITHOUT WARRANT

LIQUID MIND PUBLISHING

To eight-year-old me.
Lookit, kiddo.
We did it.

1 MARIE

MARIE LOOPED a scarf around her neck one more time as she locked her apartment door and made a quick start towards the car. It was still dark outside in the overcast early morning, and the orange streetlights provided the only light. She could tell autumn was here by the swirls of air escaping her mouth.

She stopped right under the awning, watching the trickling sprinkles of rain catch the light of the streetlamps. She bounced on the tip of her toes to get blood flowing as she patted the outside of her pockets and bag.

Keys. Check.

Wallet. Check.

Purse. Check.

Lunch. Lunch? Shoot. She forgot to pack a lunch.

Marie glanced at her watch. She could dash back, but then she wouldn't have time to grab a coffee for herself and her boss.

Coffee. I will always choose coffee.

She jogged to her Honda Pilot and got in, starting the ignition and cringing at the blare of hard rock blasting through her stereo before turning the music all way down. She then cranked the heat to full blast.

Once the heat set in and warmed her face, she pulled her scarf loose. Eyes on the rearview mirror, Marie backed out of her parking space and started the drive into town.

There weren't many people on the road at this time of morning, one of the biggest reasons she liked starting her days early. The salon she worked at opened early in the morning anyway. She thought about the customers she would have that day as she came to one of the only stoplights.

Marie drove down Main Street, eventually spotting the lights of Cobain's, the best—and only—coffee shop in town. She looked through the windows, trying to see who was working, but the rain blurred both her windows and those of the coffee shop.

She parallel parked outside the building and turned her overhead light on. She dug through her purse until she found her lipstick and opened the mirror on the driver side visor when something caught her eye through the front windshield.

Since streetlights were sparse in this part of town, the lights shining through the many windows of Cobain's and the solitary lamppost about fifty feet away were the only forms of illumination. The lamppost lit the entrance to one of the many trails in the woods surrounding Marlborough. The fact that there was a lamppost at all was proof that this one was a particularly popular hiking trail.

Popular maybe wasn't the right word. Marlborough wasn't a big town. Marie only knew of a handful of people who used the trails. It wouldn't be too surprising if someone was out there right now, but it was freezing, raining, and the clouds only seemed to be getting darker.

Marie clicked her interior overhead light off. *Had* she just seen someone walking—rather, *hobbling* towards the tree line? She squinted through the droplets on her windshield, but the warm air in the car contrasted with the cold air outside, making her windows fog up.

Could it have been...?

Marie shook her head. It's too early for this nonsense. She just needed coffee to straighten her head.

She put her lipstick away, picked up her bag, and headed inside.

The smell of freshly brewed coffee filled her nose as she opened the door. The aroma caused her mouth to water in anticipation of much needed caffeine. She unwound her scarf entirely as she made her way to the counter.

"Morning, Marie."

Kurtis, the owner, came around the corner and smiled at her as she approached the till. He was a handsome man in his late thirties with dirty, graying auburn hair and a signature flannel atop a 90s band t-shirt.

Marie blushed, as she always did whenever she was around Kurtis. "Hi, how are you?"

"Can't complain," he said, leaning over the counter. "You're one of the first in this mornin'."

"Yeah?" She tilted her head in invitation for hm to continue as she pulled her wallet out.

"Yeah, that girl who works at the grocery store... what's her name?" Kurtis scrunched his face, his shaggy hair falling into his eyes, before snapping his fingers. "Jessie. She came in to use the bathroom before going on her run. Only other person in so far."

Marie nodded, an image of her boss, Sam, styling Jessie's hair passing through her mind. "I know Jessie. She's cool. Braver than me though. I'm pretty sure that crazy homeless guy lives somewhere close to here. I thought I saw him going into the woods before I came in."

"Maybe. He comes in every now and then when it's extra cold out. I know he's kinda whack, but I feel bad for him."

"I still don't understand how he's not in jail."

Kurtis shrugged. "No idea. Anyways, what can I getcha?"

"Two large hot mochas with whip, please."

"You got it, love." Kurt rang her up, giving Marie a cheeky smile before getting busy making the coffee.

As the sound of the grinder filled the air, Marie walked over to the floor to ceiling window and tried to look out. It was still so dark outside that she couldn't see a thing without pressing her nose to the glass. Instead, she looked at her reflection in the window and noticed that one of her white sneakers was untied.

Marie bent over at the waist and tied her shoe, her bag strap falling off her shoulder. She turned her head and looked around to see if Kurtis was looking her way, fully aware he could have a good view of her butt. However, like the good barista he was, his focus was on making the coffee drinks.

Marie signed and stood, readjusting her bag and checking her other sneaker for good measure. She looked back out the window.

Around the entirety of Cobain's was a cement sidewalk, but due to the bright lights of the shop, she could only see a small portion of it and that was shiny from the rain. She watched the rain drops hitting the cement for a few minutes before a small rock rolled towards the window and tapped the edge of the frame and glass with a small *tink*.

Maybe the light wind rolled the rock across the ground? No. Did something kick it?

Marie looked up, this time cupping her hands around her eyes to look out. She could have sworn she saw something scurry back into the shadows, but—

Kurtis's reflection in the window caught her eye as he moved to the counter. Marie turned and made her way back as he raised an eyebrow at her. "Whatcha looking at?"

"I saw a rock hit the glass outside the window and I was trying to see if someone had kicked it."

"Probably a racoon. Little jerks have been making a mess around the dumpsters." Kurtis put the coffees in a carrying tray and slid it towards her, a smile forming on his lips.

Marie smiled back. "Smells divine. Thanks Kurtis."

"No problem-o, doll. Don't be a stranger."

"Am I ever?" Marie shot him with a finger gun with one hand as she picked up the coffee carrier in the other.

He winked and waved as Marie left the building.

A chill ran down her spine, an icy reminder that she had forgotten to loop her scarf back around her neck.

She walked to her car and put the coffees on the hood as she dug into her bag for her keys.

A scream almost made her drop her bag.

Marie froze.

Silence.

She turned and looked to the trail entrance. The scream had come from there, some ways off...or had it?

Maybe... maybe she was just hearing things?

Marie hesitated. It was dark and she was alone. Kurtis wouldn't be able to see her from inside.

Maybe it's just that raccoon he mentioned... though she didn't think raccoons sounded like that.

Marie wrapped her scarf back around her neck before pulling her pepper spray out of her purse. She then pulled her phone from her pocket to use the flashlight. She glanced through the windows of Cobain's, but Kurtis was no longer behind the counter. Should she go in and say something? No. What could Kurtis do? He was the only employee on duty, which meant he couldn't leave the building.

Marie walked down the side of the building in the light of the windows, holding the pepper spray as she crossed onto the path to the illuminated trailhead.

At the entrance to the woods, Marie hesitated again.

What am I doing? If she was smart, she would just leave. Isn't this how every horror movie went, or every true crime documentary started? Single woman walking alone in the woods?

Then she thought about Jessie. Jessie was a single woman alone in the woods.

But she chose this, and it sounded as if this was a norm for Jessie to go running in the morning.

Marie was going to be late for work. Her coffee was getting cold, still perched atop her car hood and exposed to the chilly air. What if she really *was* just hearing things? But then what if the roles were reversed and Marie had been the one to scream but no one came?

She could call the police, but then she imagined the conversation.

911, what's your emergency?

Yeah, I think I heard a scream coming from the woods? But I'm not sure. Could be a raccoon.

She cringed and then sighed.

She looked at the clock on her phone. If she didn't find anything in five minutes, she would leave.

Marie pulled up Cobain's number and called it.

"This is Cobain's, Kurtis speaking."

"Hey, it's Marie. I think Jessie might be in trouble."

"What? What happened?"

"I heard something coming from the woods. I'm going to go check it out."

"What, no. You should call the police."

"But something could be wrong *now*."

"Then I can go—"

"No, you can't leave the shop. I'm just going to go."

Kurtis let out an exasperated exhale. "Marie—"

"Listen, if you don't get a call from me in five minutes, call the police." Marie hung up and held the flashlight up.

The grass was dewy, and the surrounding damp dirt contained fresh footprints. Someone had walked—or hobbled—on the trail recently.

Marie started walking. She kept her eyes on the trail, listening for anything apart from her breath and footsteps, but all she could hear was the patter of rain on the trees around her. The smell of petrichor, usually so calming, did nothing to alleviate the anxiety that was growing in Marie the further into the forest she walked.

Maybe it really was nothing. I could probably turn around—

Her gaze landed on her shoes, bringing her to an abrupt halt. It was dark in the woods, and the pathway was covered in peat, so she wasn't surprised to see her sneakers were shiny with dew and covered in forest debris. But why were the tips of her shoes smeared with what looked like—

A snap of branches caused Maria to jerk her head up. She turned her flashlight towards the noise, expecting an animal to jump out. Nothing did. Ahead, between some trees off the pathway she could see something pink.

Maria felt blood begin to pound in her ears.

She made her way toward the trees, still straining to see or hear anything. Once she got there, she pushed some ferns away and looked down, blinking rain out of her eyes.

Jessie lay there, spread eagle on the ground, a pink jacket wrapped around her torso. Her eyes were rolled back in her head and her hair was wet with—was that blood on her neck?

Maria looked down Jessie's body and realized that it simply stopped, her hip bones protruding from the bottom of her torso.

Both of her legs were missing.

Maria heard another scream.

Her own.

2 WILLOW

I OPENED MY EYES, squinting against the bright sun shining through a gap in my curtains. I blinked and rolled over into a stretch.

Wait a minute.

My heart began pounding and I sat up, running the edge of my comforter through my fingers.

How did I get here? I was on my couch last night watching a movie with—

Soft clinking sounded from my kitchen and my heart started to beat faster. I sprung out of the covers, grabbed my robe from the end of my bed, and put it on.

I threw open my bedroom door and looked out at the open floor plan of my apartment.

Paxton Holt was in the kitchen, opening and closing cabinets to find what he needed to make tea.

"Good morning, sleeping beauty." He smiled at me as he poured hot water into two mugs prepared with tea bags. "I was just about to come wake you."

He was wearing lounge clothes, not quite PJs. His hazelnut brown hair was sticking up in glorious bedhead fashion. The toaster popped up with bagels and I watched as he placed them on the plate beside it.

I leaned against my bedroom door frame, my hand on my heart. "You scared me."

"Sorry. I figured I'd make us breakfast before we head to the station."

Butterflies flew through my stomach, though I wasn't sure if that was from him or the smell of the food making my stomach rumble. "Thanks. Did... did you spend the night?"

Paxton shot me the briefest glance before looking back at his task of putting another bagel in the toaster. "No. You fell asleep last night half-way through the movie, so I put you to bed and then went back to my place. Seemed rude to stay."

I was suddenly aware of how fuzzy my teeth felt. I was sorry he hadn't stayed but grateful that he hadn't been subjected to my morning breath.

I nodded. "I'm gonna go—" I pointed to the bathroom behind me with my thumb. "Be out in a minute."

Paxton nodded and started spreading cream cheese on the bagel as I turned and made my way to the small three-quarter bathroom tucked into the corner of my bedroom.

I grabbed my toothbrush and toothpaste from the glass cup beside the sink and turned the facet on. A bunch of sleepy, half-formed thoughts swirled in my head as the adrenaline in my system dissipated.

Paxton had not stayed. A disappointment.

Paxton had seen me fall asleep and put me to bed. A good thing. A sweet thing.

Just like him coming back first thing this morning to make us breakfast before we head into work together. I don't think anyone had ever made me breakfast before. Then again, no part of any bit of my relationship with him—work or otherwise—was something I had ever had before.

The case we had just solved had been a patchy start to our working together. He had not been the best teacher and I had been an even poorer student. I knew that we were going to be given a new case today and I wanted this one to go more smoothly. I would do everything I could for it to do so.

Being a consultant for the FBI was not something I ever saw for myself, yet here I was with the opportunity of a lifetime, partnered with an amazing guy.

I laughed when I caught sight of the toothpaste dribbling down my chin in the mirror.

As I finished brushing my teeth and washing my face, I heard my phone ding from my bedside table.

Curious, I came out of the bathroom and picked it up, seeing that Nicole had messaged me. I started reading the message as I walked into the living room.

Smith and I decided we're going to go on a small vacation around the Olympic Peninsula before heading East.

A clinking sound brought my attention to Paxton as he followed me into the living room, holding a tray laden with two steaming mugs of tea and two plates of cream cheese bagels and cold ham.

"You really didn't have to do this." I said, as I sank onto the couch pulling my feet into a lotus position before putting a throw pillow on my lap and tucking in to use it as a tray table for my breakfast. I took the plate Paxton handed me.

He waved his hand as he sat beside me and took a big bite. Through chews he said, "No problem. We gotta be at the office soon but we've got time."

I looked over at my clock on the stove and saw he was right.

Paxton took another bite. "I got a text from Smith this morning."

I looked up, swallowing my own bite. "Oh?"

"Apparently after we left their place last night, he and Nicole talked and decided to take a vacation before they head to Tennessee. They're going to see Smith's brother up north. Lives somewhere along the Olympic Peninsula. I guess they're leaving later today."

"Nicole texted me too. Can't say I blame them for wanting to get out of the apartment after everything."

"No kidding."

We munched on our breakfast in silence for a moment and I took a sip of tea to wash it down.

"I didn't know Smith had a brother," I said, breaking the silence.

"Me neither, actually."

I looked at him for a moment and asked, "Do you have any siblings?"

It dawned on me that, even with as much time I'd spent with Paxton over the last few months, I really didn't know much about him.

"Me?" Paxton wiped his mouth with a napkin and shook his head. "Nah, I'm an only child. What about you?"

I shrugged, rubbing my fingers together to rid them of crumbs. "I actually don't know."

Paxton and I held each other's gaze for an extra second, his features lined with understanding.

We sat in silence for a few more minutes after that, finishing our food and tea. I noticed he had opened my blinds and the sun streamed in through the blades, creating a zebra of light on the floor. I was mostly moved into my new apartment now. Almost all the boxes were unpacked and stacked neatly on the tile by the front door. How Paxton managed to secure the unit across from his still boggled me, but the commute to spend time together was convenient.

It was nice to know he was there. Leaving my little house in the woods had been hard, and I was still adjusting to all the changes. I hadn't heard from Malcome in a while and had put a pause on all my personal one-on-one counseling sessions I gave until I was properly settled. It was a lot to process, but Paxton helped me feel safe in my new sanctuary. In my new life.

"You don't have to ask, you know." I straightened my leg out, touching his thigh with my foot.

Paxton paused halfway through stacking our empty plates back on the tray. He raised his mug and eyebrows, a silent request for me to elaborate.

I felt the butterflies in my stomach again. Definitely not food related now. "If you ever want to spend the night. You... you don't have to ask. And you don't have to sleep on the couch either." I worked to keep my breathing even as I waited for his response. I don't think either of us are used to that level of boldness from me.

The corner of his lips twitched. His gray eyes arrested me as he looked at me over his mug. "Noted."

I forced myself to hold his gaze. His hair had fallen onto his forehead. I wanted to reach over and brush it away, but he had never liked when I had done that in the past. I settled for reaching over and putting my hand on his knee. We *did* have time before we were needed at the bureau—

I jumped as both our phones buzzed, interrupting what could have been a moment.

Paxton looked at me. "Office?"

I looked back at him. "Case update?"

"Real clothes?"

"You drive?"

"Let's go."

Forty-five minutes later, we walked through the parking garage into the elevator that led to the bureau. Paxton pressed the button for our floor, and I enjoyed the rushing feeling of traveling upwards. It always smelled like a mixture of sub sandwiches and feet.

"A new case already," I said.

"It ebbs and flows. I guess we're in a bit of flow state," Paxton said as he watched the small screen above the floor buttons change. "I know we already talked about this, but I want you to know that I'm sorry for being hard on you during our last investigation. It was your first one, so it was bound to be a learning curve. I should have had...well...more—"

"Grace?"

"Exactly."

We both chuckled and I realized that was something I liked about him: he understood my humor.

"I'm not much for partners," he said. "Never have been. But you're different. You know your stuff. And I trust you. That's something I don't say often."

I felt butterflies again. I know I'm trustworthy, but to have it confirmed by the person I trust more than anyone else had me relieved.

"If I didn't say it before, I just want you to know I'm glad you're here... with me." His pinky finger brushed mine. "I'll do better in the future."

"So will I." I wrapped my pinky around his. "You can count on me."

The elevator dinged and the moment was over. The doors opened and he unlatched his pinky from mine.

We walked onto our unit's floor, a large room filled with cubicles. I squinted at the contrast between the soft orange light in the elevator to the white, fluorescent lighting. The room smelled of coffee, fresh printer ink, and a slight hint of damp clothing.

We each nodded our greetings at the other agents as we headed directly to the director's office. I waved at Agent Brown as we passed his desk, his acknowledgement coming in the form of a raised coffee mug. Paxton knocked on the door and a firm, "Come in," followed from the other side.

We walked in to see Marcus McCannon's stoicism reflected inside. I looked around the room, noting his tidy space was the same as ever. Shelves lined the right wall and filing cabinets lined the wall next to it. He had a single personal picture on one of the shelves, that of two young teenagers holding baseball equipment and grinning, their teeth covered in braces. I appreciated that McCannon kept his personal and professional life separate, especially in this line of work. I glanced at Paxton and fought an ironic grin.

McCannon's clear redwood desk, devoid of any personal touches or even stacks of papers, faced the window that had a view of the rest of the office, the blinds lowered but open. Two square but comfortable chairs sat in front of his desk.

"Grace. Holt." McCannon glanced up from the file in front of him as we walked in, his cyan eyes piercing as they looked at us over his glasses. He ran a hand through his graying chestnut hair. "Have a seat."

I sank into the worn leather of the left chair. Paxton settled in on my right.

McCannon sat forward, resting his interlocked fingers on the edge of his desk. "Excellent job on the Hourglass Killer case. The guy got what he deserved. Couldn't have done it without either of you," he said. If we didn't know him as well as we did, the comment would have seemed perfunctory. We knew better: McCannon was not one to hand out praise lightly.

I felt my face flush as Paxton said, "Thank you, sir."

I cast another glance at Paxton, remembering his arm in a sling, and him holding a bouquet of roses. That night had been horrible, but the aftermath hadn't been so bad.

"Now, new assignment."

Paxton got out his notebook and pen and I sat up straighter, shaking off the memories of seeing my friend tied up and the jarring sound of gunshots, and gave all my attention to McCannon. I noticed then that he rolled his shoulders and realized that his demeanor was grimmer than normal.

"We received a call earlier from Chief Alvarado. Runs a department in a small town about an hour from here. Found a body earlier this morning. Thought maybe we'd be interested in lending a hand."

"Didn't notify the state troopers?" Paxton asked.

"They did. And *they* were told to notify us. This victim was found along one of the local hiking trails. They found a stab wound in her jugular."

"Still not seeing why it falls in our lap," Paxton said.

"Both her legs were removed."

Paxton and I looked at each other before I said, "Her *legs* were removed?"

"This woman wasn't just killed but severely mutilated."

"Do we have any case notes yet?" Paxton asked.

"They sent over a digital file. I sent it to both of your emails just before you arrived."

I tapped on my phone and saw the message from McCannon sitting at the top of my inbox. I clicked it open, seeing that a PDF file and several JPEGs awaited. I clicked on the first image. What I saw nearly brought up the breakfast Paxton had made me.

"Not for the faint of heart." McCannon's faced betrayed no sign of emotion.

"This is... diabolical. Monstrous." I swallowed down the taste of bile in my throat.

"Couldn't have been an animal attack," Paxton said. "Those cuts are too clean to be anything other than premeditated. ID on the victim?"

"None as of yet, at least not that they've shared. No doubt they're working on it now. They'll fill you in more when you get down to Marlborough."

"Marlborough," I enunciated the word. "I've never heard of that place, have you?" I turned to Paxton and was surprised to see he had stiffened.

"Yep."

"You know it?" I asked him. I noticed he had begun tapping his pen against his leg, something he only does when he's agitated.

Paxton nodded. "I lived there for a time, when I was in training post-college."

I raised my eyebrows. "I didn't know that."

"I've lived in Seattle most of my life, but I uh... had a short stint in Marlborough."

"Then you're familiar with the layout." McCannon leaned back in his chair. "I recommend getting a room out there. Be better than commuting every day. I already spoke to the chief. He'll be expecting you."

3 WILLOW

THE SOUND of my heels clicking on the pavement enveloped my mind as I followed Paxton through the parking garage to his car. The scent of exhaust was potent as usual. I watched Paxton's stride before my eyes landed on the back of his head.

I was puzzled.

I had seen Paxton facing the worst of humanity. I had seen him standing calm and brave in the face of death. And yet the mere mention of the town *Marlborough* had been enough for all the blood to drain from his face.

We got into the car, Paxton in the driver's seat and I the shotgun. I pulled up Marlborough on my phone's GPS. Fifty-eight minutes northwest from here. "I've been in Washington nearly all my life, but I've never heard of Marlborough." Granted, growing up in a cult does tend to limit one's grasp of local geography.

Paxton grunted as he put his seatbelt on. "I'm not surprised. It's a small town. You either grew up there or pass through on the interstate and forget the name as soon as it shrinks in your review mirror."

"Guess you're the rare outlier since you fall in neither of those categories." Usually a quip like that would have gotten a chuckle out of him, but Paxton didn't reply.

I looked over at him, feeling a slight twinge of anxiety flare at his change in mood. I decided to change subjects. "I don't know about you, but I could do with a cup of coffee. After we pack a bag, wanna get a pick-me-up before we head that way?"

"Sounds like a plan." His tone was calm, but his knuckles on the steering wheel had gone white.

I reached over and grabbed the hand he had resting on his knee.

We'd gotten more comfortable with physical affection over the last few weeks. We shared kisses, held hands, and he'd even fallen asleep with his head in my lap during a previous movie night.

But that was all. Nothing further. Even when we had had the perfect opportunity last night.

I knew I was ready to take the next step in our relationship. I told him I wanted to take it slow, but maybe not *this* slow.

Something was holding him back. I couldn't place my finger on why he remained so reserved and guarded. His movements were always careful, never once going beyond what was appropriate.

Like now. He held my hand back, rubbing his thumb across my knuckles. But I would have preferred if his hand traveled over to my upper thigh.

I contented myself with squeezing his hand. I *was* ready for the next step, but I was nervous too. Maybe he had reason to be more nervous than me.

We made it back to our complex. I ran up to my apartment and packed a bag. I grabbed enough clothing to last a week, my toiletries, and my laundry detergent.

Field work was often messy.

Field work at crime scenes even more so.

I hauled my things to the door as a quick knock sounded. Paxton opened it when I said, "Come in." A gym bag was slung over his shoulder. His eyes remained soft as he grabbed my bag from me and slung it over his other shoulder.

I closed the door behind us, glancing at my security camera/doorbell I had installed on my door. I made sure it was on, locked my door, and started to walk away. But I froze and turned to look back at my door.

Had I locked it?

I know I had. I *just* did.

But the urge to double check was too strong. I looked down the hall to see Paxton's head disappearing down the stairwell.

I put my key in my lock again, unlocked the door, opened it, closed it, and turned the key again. I lightly jostled the door handle, nodded, and turned.

But had I *really* locked it?

What on earth was going on? Why was I feeling so paranoid?

I turned around and looked at the door. It looked the same as I had left it seven seconds ago. I shook my head and walked to the end of the hall.

But what if I hadn't *really* locked it? What if someone pushed all the way down on the handle and the door opened?

I stopped at the top of the stairs.

I had already checked the door. I couldn't check it again. We were in a hurry. I had already checked it. *I had already checked it.*

But what if I hadn't?

I spun on my heal and marched to my door. I slowly put my key in, turned it all the way to the right, opened the door, shut the door, turned the key all the way to the left, heard the click of the lock. I pushed all the way down on the handle and shook the door. It didn't move.

"Willow?"

I turned my head to see Paxton jogging down the hall to me, hands still on my keys and door handle. "What are you doing? Did you forget something?"

"I couldn't remember if I locked the door or not."

He watched me try to open door. "It seems good. Let's go."

I followed him down the hall but stopped. What if I hadn't turned the key in the lock all the way and now the lock was only partially deployed?

I wanted to scream. I had already checked the lock! I couldn't take my key *out* of the keyhole if the lock was only partially deployed. This was stupid, silly, why—

"Willow?" Paxton came up to me, his brows furrowed. I could tell he was getting annoyed. "What's going on? We gotta go."

"What if I didn't lock the door?" The words tumbled out of my mouth in a whisper, and I felt a blush creep up my cheeks at how ludicrous it sounded.

Concern flashed over Paxton's face. He took a step closer, looking between both my eyes before his brow relaxed. He looked back at my door then at me.

"It's not about the door, is it?"

I looked down.

He took a step closer to me. "This is the first time you've left your new home for any length of time."

I shifted my shoulder, stretching my head to the side.

"Hey." He took my hand in one of his and with the other one he made me look at him by pushing my head up with a crooked finger under my chin. "It's okay. I know this is hard for you. But it'll be okay. This apartment is safe. You are safe."

I looked between his gray eyes. The look there was still reserved, but it was accompanied by an adamancy and laced with tenderness.

I felt some of the tension leave my shoulders. I nodded.

He gently extricated my keys from my clamped fingers, walked to my door, and locked it. "There. I have made positively sure that the door is locked. No one's getting in."

The incessant need to continue to check had vanished the minute he took my keys. I nodded at him again.

He took my hand and we made our way downstairs.

I sipped on my hot dirty chai in the passenger seat as we left the outskirts of Seattle. The aroma of spices helped me settle in for the drive. Paxton sipped his hot black coffee. I wondered about his time in Marlborough. Why had he lived out there? What had caused him to move away?

And why hadn't he told me about it before?

I was looking at the rain drops sliding at a steep slant on my passenger side window when my phone buzzed inside my purse. I took it out to look at it and the contact name lighting up the screen had me grinning. "It's a message from Cory."

"Megan's aunt, right?"

I put my cup in the cup holder. "That's right. She said: *I just got Megan a*

*phone for her birthday. She's getting ready to videocall you. I wanted to give
you a heads-up."*

And right on cue, my phone started ringing with an unknown number. I
tilted my body so that Paxton could see my phone screen too. I felt a flash of
trepidation at answering an unknown number, but when I swiped right to
answer the call, a bundle of white fur covered most of the screen. In the
upper left corner, Megan's sweet grin greeted me.

"Megan! It's so good to see you."

"Hi Willow. I got a new phone and I wanted to show you Sapphire."

"The phone's too close, silly, back up a bit so Willow can see you." I heard
Cory laugh in the background.

"Oops." I got a view of Megan's chin as she picked the phone up and set it
against something before scootching back into frame. She was sitting on the
floor on her knees, one arm under a white adolescent cat, the other brushing
her curly brown hair out of her face.

Paxton glanced over from the road long enough to get a look at our friend
on the phone. "Wow, Sapphire's gotten so big."

"Is that Agent Holt?" I heard Cory say, her voice getting louder as she got
closer to the camera.

"Mhmm." Megan looked up at her aunt as Cory's head popped into
frame in the upper right corner of my phone.

"Hi, you two." Cory smiled at us.

"Hey Cory." Paxton waved.

"On another job?"

"We are," I said. "But we have a few minutes."

"Megan, why don't you tell Willow and Agent Holt what happened
today in school?"

Megan, still sitting on the floor trying to keep Sapphire from escaping,
gave her aunt a sheepish grin before looking at us. "I got an A on my science
test today."

"Heck yeah, air high-five," Paxton said and Megan giggled as they "high-
fived" over video.

"That's amazing Megan! You keep up the good work. Agent Holt and I
are proud of you."

Megan nodded, her hair falling in her face. She pushed it back with one hand but that allowed Sapphire to break free. Megan jumped up and ran out of frame.

"Oh, that girl," Cory said as she sat on the couch in front of the phone.

"How are things?" I asked her.

"Much better than the last time we chatted. Megan seems to be adjusting well. She even has a playdate with a little girl in her art class this weekend."

"That kind of interaction will be good for her."

A crash came from the background.

Cory let out an exasperated sigh. "That damn cat. I gotta go make sure that wasn't something irreplaceable."

I laughed. "Say bye to Megan for us."

Cory rolled her eyes, but she smiled. "Will do. Bye you two."

"Bye," Paxton and I said in unison and the screen went dark.

"It was good to see them both," I said, picking my chai up again.

Paxton nodded. "You know if it weren't for her, we wouldn't be here now."

"On our way to a crime scene?"

"No." Paxton shot me a look filled with meaning. "We wouldn't be here *together* on our way to a crime scene."

I laughed as butterflies erupted in my stomach for the third time that morning. "Shut up and drive, Romeo."

We smiled at each other. I reveled in the shared trust we had for one another. In that moment everything was right.

Until something flickered over Paxton's face. The smile vanished, and he moved his hand back to the steering wheel, turning his gaze back towards the road.

The happiness I felt morphed into consternation.

Had I done something? What wasn't he telling me?

4   HOLT

I HAD NEVER WANTED to go back to Marlborough again. And certainly not with Willow.

The drive from Seattle was as beautiful as I remembered. The evergreens were right up to the interstate on each side, so tall you could only see them, the sky, and the road. Rain pattered against the windshield as we drove deeper into the Olympic Peninsula. I had the heat on low, wanting Willow to be warm and my fingers to not be icicles.

I had kept both my hands on the steering wheel, but Willow had reached her arm over the center counsel and was slowly rubbing the back of her fingers up and down my triceps as she looked at the case file on her phone.

I glanced over at her. She had that cute little crease between her brows that only appeared when she was concentrating.

I had to stop myself from letting out an exasperated sigh. I didn't want to take her to Marlborough. I didn't want my past to be linked to her. I didn't want her to know.

Twenty minutes later, we were entering the outskirts of Marlborough.

Per our instructions, we pulled into a spot in front of Cobain's, an old two-story building that housed the local favorite coffee shop inside. The parking lot was small and filled with local police cars. The outside of the building was mostly wood and windows, like a chic fishbowl cabin. With how crooked the exterior walls were, I had forever been surprised it had passed inspections. I hadn't seen the place in years. I wasn't really happy to again.

"Looks like the whole PD is here," Willow said as we both got out.

I rolled my tight shoulders, shutting the door behind me. "Yep. This is going to be ugly. You ready for this?"

Willow took a deep breath as she shrugged into her trench coat. "It's what we're here for."

I followed her past the coffee shop. I caught sight of my reflection in the window of the entrance as we passed it and remembered the last time I had opened that door. I felt the back of my throat start to hurt from straining to keep the feelings at bay. I clenched my jaw and shook the memory of echoing laughter out of my mind.

We made our way up to the trail entrance leading to the crime scene. A line of yellow tape spanned between the trees, blocking the pathway entrance. A young officer with baby blue eyes and a thick, dark mustache stood on the outside of the tape by a solitary lamp post, arms crossed in front of him. He raised his eyebrows when he saw us, but Willow and I both held up our badges. "FBI. I'm Agent Holt and this is Dr. Grace."

The officer nodded and raised the tape to let us pass underneath, his face inexpressive. "We've been awaiting your arrival."

Willow and I ducked under the tape. The officer handed us some latex gloves and gestured for us to follow him. The trees were not so close together that the woods felt wild and unexplored, but it was darker under the thickening canopy of branches. I glanced at Willow, expecting her to show as many nerves as I felt, but she looked calm and collected. I remembered she preferred being outside than indoors. She glanced at me and I saw warmth in her expression.

I looked away.

After walking a few minutes, we came to a tiny clearing beside the pathway. More crime scene tape was wrapped around the surrounding trees. A neatly squared off area. If this was a homicide, this was the perfect place for it.

A half-dozen officers were milling around, some taking pictures, others taking notes or walking around, looking through the underbrush with flashlights and evidence bags in hand.

In the epicenter of the trees, damp from the rain, lay the body.

Most of it.

I sensed Willow stiffen beside me as we walked closer.

The officer who had guided us stopped behind a large man in a brown uniform and tapped his shoulder. "Chief? The feds are here."

The large man turned, his thumbs in his belt hoops and my first impression was to not get on the bad side of this guy. He was about my height but twice as broad. His eyes and 5 o'clock shadow were both a deep black.

"Ah, you must be Agent Holt and Professor Grace." His voice came through in a deep rumble. He nodded as the young officer left before reaching out to shake Willow's hand. He exuded confidence and efficiency. "I'm Chief Weston Alvarado. Wish we could have met under more pleasant circumstances."

"Likewise," I said as he shook my hand next.

"It takes an aberrant person to kill someone," Chief Alvarado said as Willow and I moved to either side of him. "But this? Can either of you tell me why in the *hell* this woman is missing both of her legs?"

We looked down at the body. A young blonde woman, likely in her mid-to-late twenties lay on her back. She was wearing a light pink winter jacket over a white long-sleeve shirt and black leggings. Her arms were splayed up by her head which was turned to the side. A huge slash ran across her throat. The blood had run down her neck and stained the front of her shirt and jacket. Etched into her skin around the stab wound on her neck was a symbol:

Even laying on mulch, the blood had pooled under her head. My eyes traveled down the length of her torso to see it had also pooled under her hips.

Both of her legs were missing. My mind kept wanting to fill in the gaps, where human legs should be.

I swore under my breath when I caught sight of her hip bone.

On top of her chest lay a completed corner section of a puzzle. The chief and I both knelt down to get a better look. There wasn't enough of the puzzle built to tell what the completed picture would be, but the section visible looked to be the bottom corner depicting red lines over a blue backdrop.

"Cause of death is either the laceration to the jugular or bleeding out. Believe this young lady's been dead since between six and six-thirty this morning. She was found by Marie, that young lady over there." He pointed behind him. Two officers stood with a young raven-haired woman sitting on a fallen log. Her face was ashen as if she was ready to throw up. Maybe she already had.

We all turned back to the corpse. Willow walked around the victim's body and knelt to examine her head.

"No documented ID found on her, but this young woman's name is"— The chief cleared his throat—"*Was* Jessie Lee. She worked at the local grocery. Everyone knew her. Sweet girl."

Willow examined the woman's torso. "You said Marie found her. How did she find Jessie's body in the first place?"

"She said she was at Cobain's to pick up coffee and heard something coming from the woods. Came to investigate."

The corner of Willow's mouth flickered downward, an expression I had seen a few times before. It was an indication of her concern for the woman's safety.

"Has she been interviewed yet?" I asked.

"She was distressed earlier, so it was hard to get a cohesive word out of her. She's calmed down a bit now though." Chief Alvarado stood and gestured for us to follow him.

We followed the chief towards Marie. She glanced up at us and her chest started to rise and fall a little faster. I removed my gloves and stuffed them into my jacket pocket as I extricated my notepad and pen.

I opened my mouth to start asking her questions, but Willow began first.

She squatted down so that she was eye-level with the woman, keeping her balance by putting her hand on the log next to her.

"Hi." Her tone was soothing and warm. I could feel my own shoulders relaxing, the way they usually do whenever Willow speaks. "My name's Willow and this is my partner, Agent Holt. We're with the FBI. I understand your name is Marie?"

The woman nodded. "Yes, my name is Marie. And before you ask, I was the one who found... her." Her whole body shuddered as she glanced towards the mutilated body in the small clearing.

"I know this is difficult for you, but I'm going to need you to answer some questions for me. Can you do that?"

"They already asked me a bajillon questions. Please don't make me live through it again." Marie closed her eyes tight, and tears rolled down her face, making little dark circles on her jeans.

Willow was silent for a minute. "Were you two friends?"

Marie let out a soft wet chuckle. "No. Friend*ly*. She was nice. She got her hair cut at our salon. We went to high school together. Nothing beyond that."

I started taking notes.

"It still must have been hard for you to find her like that."

Marie's face contorted again. "It was awful. I almost left her out here, left without checking. When I heard that scream in the woods..."

Willow waited a moment for Marie to collect her thoughts before continuing. "Did you see anything strange?"

Marie glanced up at the officers on either side of her. "I thought I saw a figure at the trail head entrance when I was heading into Cobain's this morning but that's not unusual. People love to hike here, but..." she bit her bottom lip.

"But what?" Willow asked.

"There's this homeless man rumored to live somewhere here in the woods. And when I saw the figure entering the woods, I... I thought it might have been him."

"Ol' Tony?" One of the officers raised an eyebrow. "He's a little weird to be sure, but—"

"He's not just *a little weird*." Marie's face went from ashen to red as her angered flared. "He's crazy. We all know he's one of *them*."

"One of who?" I looked down at Willow and saw my own confusion reflected in her face.

"I can fill you in later," The chief said under his breath to us. "Marie, he was acquitted—"

"We all know he helped *do* that to all those poor people!"

"Marie—"

"He *knows* what happened to Jessie, dammit. Why won't you *listen* to me?" Marie's angry tears flowed down her cheeks as she started to stand.

"Hey." Willow stood and placed a gentle hand on Marie's shoulder, forcing the young woman to look at her. "*I'm* listening to you. We're going to find out what happened to Jessie."

The fight melted out of Marie and she nodded, sitting back down. She rested her head in her hands and shook with soft sobs.

Chief Alvarado nodded to us and led us back up the path.

"This is strange," Willow's brow furrowed. "Seems like we should find this Tony guy and ask him some questions."

"No other person of interest?" I asked the chief. "No boyfriend?"

The chief took his hat off and ran his hand through his military cropped black hair before putting the hat back on his head. "We're double checking but nothing that we're aware of. Right now, Tony is top of the list."

5 FIFTEEN YEARS AGO

WHERE WAS MOTHER?

He got up from his little rug in the living room, leaving the puzzle from Mother unfinished, all the homemade wooden pieces scattered about. He was hungry and wanted some of her freshly made bread. But he wasn't allowed to cut the loaf himself when she wasn't there. A silly rule, but a firm one none-theless.

Knives are tools. Tools can hurt when you aren't careful with them. That's what she liked to say to him. *Pain must only be caused for a purpose.*

So where was she?

He looked all around their cabin. She wasn't anywhere.

"Mother?" He said out loud, just to be sure.

No response. Mr. Tony wasn't there either.

He meandered into the kitchen and looked at the bread on the counter. He could smell it through the box she kept it in, that wonderful yeasty golden smell. He felt his mouth water. If he got it out, was very, very careful with the knife, and cleaned everything back up, she need never know that he had gotten a slice.

It was dark inside the cabin. The candles weren't lit and the fire was dying. The sky was overcast and what little light came from the heavens had a hard time trickling through the forest their community lived in.

He rubbed his fingers against his palms, deliberating. He knew how to use a knife, had done it a million times. Mother and Mr. Tony had been very careful and thorough in teaching him. Yet he hesitated, feeling a frustrated anger rise within him. One doesn't disobey their parents lightly. If it was a pattern, children would be taken in front of the Limbless Ones.

And your Age of Abdication could be lowered.

He frowned. All he wanted was a piece of bread. And at 13 years old, he wasn't a child anymore.

Right as he started reaching for a knife, his eyes fell on the calendar hanging on the cabinet above the breadbox.

Today was Ritual Day.

Of course. That's where Mother was. It was her turn to be present at the Ritual. She had been selected as the Prayerful Bridge, whatever that meant.

"It's a huge honor," Mother had told him. "I have been selected to be in the presence of the Bloodless One. I am to be his Prayerful Bridge."

He'd had a strange feeling in his chest when she had said that to him. One of fear and excitement.

"You'll get to see The Bloodless One?"

"Yes, my precious. Let us hope he rises soon. He still requires the Perfect Pieces to be resurrected."

He looked out the window and saw the little village was empty. If he stood on his toes he could just make out the temple.

That's where she was.

Maybe he could go watch the ritual. The other boys had told him about a place you could watch the goings on of the inner sanctum. Temple had been built against a large tree. It was rumored among the children that the Bloodless One rested at its roots. The boys had told him that if you climbed to the right branch, you could climb onto the ledge of the building and there was a small secret space that you could climb into that overlooked the altar.

He'd never done it. When he was younger, he'd been too nervous.

He would never forget the time that he had seen the oldest boy in the village, the biggest and the meanest of all of them, climb down from that secret place. That boy, not knowing he was being watched, had dropped to the ground and landed on all fours. All the blood had drained from his face and he had been crying. From that day, her boy had never been the same.

Yes, what had happened to the other boy had rattled him. But now? Now he was curious.

What *did* a ritual look like? It had been a long, long time since the last ritual day. What had that boy seen?

It couldn't be that bad. She was there. Mother wouldn't go where it was scary. Besides. He wasn't a child anymore. He shouldn't be afraid of anything. He *wasn't* afraid of anything.

He slid into his boots and grabbed his jacket before he quietly opened the front door.

Not a soul could he see. No one was supposed to be outside on Ritual Days. The door was closing behind him when he stopped.

This was worse than using a knife when Mother wasn't around. What if he got caught? What if he was taken to the Limbless Ones?

He felt a sly rebellion form in his chest.

All the priests were in the temple. And anyone who saw him would be admitting that they were out of bounds too. Fools.

He ran to the temple, then followed the other boy's instructions and climbed to the right branch. He climbed onto the ledge of the building and froze when he heard a horrific scream come from inside the temple.

A woman's scream.

Heart thudding from shock, he crawled along the edge of the roof until he saw the opening to the crawl space. He clambered into it, blinking as the light changed from the brightness of the outside to the firelight of the inside. He came to the edge of the secret space and looked down.

He felt blood start to pound in his ears and his upper lip begin to sweat. His community members surrounded the altar, swaying and chanting. He looked at the faces, recognizing the Limbless Ones, those who walked the forest, and Mr. Tony.

Mr. Tony was an unusual man. He was one of the few adults, like Mother, who had all five points to his body by the Bloodless One's command. That was only because he was the medicine man in the village. Mr. Tony had been kind to him and Mother, ever since she had decided to take him in some time ago.

Now, Mr. Tony looked strained. Sweat was pouring down his face, glistening in the firelight.

Sitting next to Mr. Tony was...

Mother leaned far back in her chair. Sweat also poured down her face, drenching her hair. She held her right hand over her left shoulder, the white fabric under her fingertips becoming dark and wet.

One of the priests carried her entire left arm to the alter. He realized beneath her hand was where her shoulder should have connected to her arm. His breathing became labored while his mind began to process an entire part of his mother was missing. The priest placed the severed limb upon the alter, bowing as he did so.

"May this offering from our Prayerful Bridge be the piece you need to be resurrected, oh Bloodless One!"

Bile rose in his throat and he swallowed it back down to keep from vomiting. He watched a small smile form on his mother's lips as she sank lower in her chair. Even in the firelight he could tell that she was ghostly pale, the stain from her left shoulder only darkening. A puddle formed on the floor beside her, dripping from her left shoulder, glistening in the firelight from the torches.

Mr. Tony was bent over her, a finger to her throat as he carved the sign into her skin.

If the Bloodless One was pleased with her offering, she would live and He'd be one step closer to being resurrected.

The priests all watched Mother and Mr. Tony. He watched as the crease between Mr. Tony's eyes became more and more pronounced. His mother's eyes were drooping.

No.

No.

No.

The Bloodless One *had* to accept her offering! She was faithful!

Mother slumped in her chair, her head rolling back, her eyes opened and blank. Mr. Tony shook his head.

"No!"

He flung himself over the edge of the hiding space and tumbled to the ground of the temple, some ten feet below. He slammed into the ground, all his weight landing on his left shoulder.

Everyone in the room looked at him in surprise, some holding their knives up. He jumped up and ran to the altar and snatched his mother's arm, running it back to her. Her arm was still warm. He felt bile burn in the back of his throat again.

"Piece her back together," he said. "If the Bloodless One doesn't want her offering, then he can make her alright again! She's been faithful! She's the Prayerful Bridge!"

"Kid!" Mr. Tony pulled him aside as a roar from the Limbless Ones rose through the temple. "You dare desecrate the temple! You dare touch even the unworthy offering to the Bloodless One?"

"Grab him!" The chief Limbless One screamed. "Perhaps the boy's offering will better please Him."

"Run!" Mr. Tony grabbed him by his shirt collar and threw him to the temple doors. "Run and don't look back!"

He ran. He ran through the village as a bell started to ring. The community started opening their doors and watching in alarm as he ran up the hilly gravel road and into the woods.

Tears streamed down his face and his vision was blurred. He could still feel the warmth of Mother's arm in his hands, the feel of her hand flopping back and forth as he had run to her side.

The sun was setting. He had no idea where he was going.

But he didn't look back.

6 WILLOW

WE ALL LOOKED over at the sound of approaching footsteps. They belonged to the cop who'd lead us to the crime scene.

"Chief," he said, "The coffee shop owner is at the tape. Wants to talk to you."

"Thanks, Lox." The chief held his hand up and we started walking back up the trail head, Lox running ahead.

"Do you think he might have seen something?" I asked, wiping away a big raindrop that had fallen into my eye.

"If nothing else, Kurtis might help us locate Tony," Chief Alvarado said. "He knows everyone."

As we got closer to the taped-off entrance, a handsome man in a flannel over an old band t-shirt came into view. His features were calm, but he was shifting his weight from foot to foot in the grass, snapping his fingers to an unknown tempo.

"Hey Kurtis," Alvarado said as he held the tape up for me and Paxton to walk under.

"Hey Chief."

"Allow me to introduce Agent Holt and Dr. Grace. They're with the FBI."

"Pleasure," Kurtis said as he shook our hands. He looked back at the chief. "How is Marie? I assume she's with you because her car's still here."

"She's distraught," I said. "I assume you're aware of the situation?"

Kutis nodded and gestured towards the deputy standing at the trail entrance. "He came and told me to close down shop to minimize tampering with the crime scene. But Marie, she's not hurt?"

"No. But finding a mutilated body takes a toll on you."

Kurtis ran his hands over his eyes. "I saw her. Jessie, I mean. She came in to use the bathroom and refill her water bottle before starting her run."

"What time was that?" Paxton asked, pulling out his notebook.

"I'm not sure. I had only just unlocked the doors a little while before, but she was the first one in. Cobain's opens at 5:30 am."

"And you didn't see anything? Anything or anyone out of the ordinary?" Paxton asked. I noted that he was hitting his pen against his leg again.

"No, sir, not a thing."

"Marie seems convinced that a homeless man by the name Tony might give us some insight," I said, noting the chief's slight unconvinced head shake. "Do you know anything about that?"

Kurtis pulled one side of his mouth down while furrowing his brow. "Old Tony? Why, did she confirm she saw him?"

"She thinks she might have," Paxton said. "Nothing at present is confirmed."

Kurtis puffed his cheeks out as he exhaled, looking perplexed. "She said as much this morning when she came in to order. I mean, I don't know much about him other than... you know."

Paxton and I exchanged looks at that. We were definitely in the dark, but Kurtis continued.

"He comes into the coffee shop sometimes. He's always polite, gets the same thing—medium hot vanilla breve."

"How often would you say he comes into the coffee shop?" The chief asked.

"I discount breves every Tuesday morning from 8-10 am. I usually see him then. If I'm allowed to open my shop again tomorrow, might be a chance he'll come in."

Kurtis shot the chief a worried look before he patted Kurtis on the shoulder. "Don't worry, you should be able to open up tomorrow. We're finishing some things up here and we'll clear out."

Some of the tension eased out of Kurtis's shoulders. "Thanks, Chief."

"We'll come in tomorrow and see if he shows up," Paxton said.

I felt my mouth contort into a frown. "If he had something to do with what happened, he probably won't show up."

"No, but it would be worth checking. Does Tony have any friends in the area?"

Kurtis shrugged. "Pretty much a loner from what I've seen. Chief, do you need Marie anymore? Her car is boxed in by all the cruisers, so I could take her home if she wants."

"Sure. I want to talk to her and let her know she'll need to come to the station to make an official statement. I'll bring her to you."

Kurtis nodded at all of us and headed back to the coffee shop.

Chief Alvarado turned to me and Paxton. "Anything you guys need, we'll make sure you have access to."

"Thank you, Chief," Paxton shook the chief's hand before he turned back towards the forest.

Sometime later, Paxton and I started walking down to our car. The rain had ceased, but now the wind had picked up. A chill went down my back as the cool air blew against the residual raindrops.

I rubbed the side of my head with a finger as we made our way through the parking lot. I felt slightly queasy. I'd seen death before. Hell, I had *killed* before. But this was different.

Seeing that poor girl, just lying there, throat stabbed and missing both of her legs. I had seen her hip bones, just exposed to the air. That was a level of grim intimacy I hoped to never share with anyone again.

What was the point of taking both of her limbs from her body? And what was that symbol?

As we got in the vehicle and put our seat belts on, I noticed Paxton's jaw was clenched shut. His knuckles were bloodless as he turned the car on and got the heat blowing.

"It bothered me too," I said.

He glanced at me but didn't hold eye contact. He shook his head. "Some *Welcome Back* to Marlborough." He pulled out and started driving back up the main road.

We rode for a few minutes in silence. I listened to the tires splashing through puddles as I held my fingers up to warm in front of the vents.

Finally, I asked the question that'd been in the back of my mind all day. "When did you live in Marlborough before?"

Paxton kept his eyes on the road. "I didn't really. I commuted back and forth to Seattle almost every day. In the end, I decided it would be better to move back to the city."

He was evading me. I didn't want to force a confidence from him, but he'd never been this on edge before.

Just when I thought we were getting on the same page and moving in the same direction, something else presented itself, leaving me scratching my head. I wanted to love this man, but something was holding him back. Was it a something I had done? Did he not trust me?

I sighed, feeling hurt that he wouldn't open up more, but also frustrated with myself for feeling that way. All I could respond with was, "I understand."

"I didn't enjoy my time living in Marlborough before, okay? I don't wanna talk about it." Paxton snapped.

And then I felt nettled. "I said I understand, Paxton."

"Good." He refused to look at me.

We drove to the motel in tense silence.

Paxton parked in front of The Glades motel, a long single-story building that looked dated but well-maintained. All the room doors were on the exterior of the building, the white backside of the curtains drawn over all the windows. The parking lot looked recently painted, the white lines separating each parking space bright, straight, and fresh, and few oil stains marred the inexpensive asphalt. We simultaneously got out of the car and walked into the lobby together.

A girl, probably about nineteen, sat behind the front desk. She looked up at us over black framed glasses, smacking a piece of lime green gum.

"Can I help you?" she asked. She wore her light brown hair in a sweat-band and ponytail and an unflattering polo with *The Glades* stitched on the left breast.

Paxton stepped up to the counter, resting his weight against his hands. "Hi, I booked two rooms under Holt?"

She glanced between the two of us and started clacking on her keyboard.

I rested my left hip against the counter and looked around the room. The lobby had a hideous runner rug that ran from the entrance to the front desk. The reception desk was along the left wall from the entrance. The door leading to the inner sanctum of the hotel was along the left side of the parallel wall and a small complimentary coffee bar stood in the right corner. A worn green couch sat desolate against the right wall. I looked at the ceiling corners and didn't see any cameras.

I felt my palms begin to sweat. The lack of even basic security didn't do any favors for my already anxious mind.

"And there you are, keys for adjacent rooms 116 and 117."

I winced, glancing around the lobby again to make sure it was empty. Receptionists were not supposed to say the room number out loud.

"By the way." I turned back at the girl's words and saw the she was giving a somewhat beady look at Holt. "Holt... you wouldn't happen to be—"

"Nope, not me. Thanks for all your help." Paxton swiped the keys off the counter and stuffed them in his pocket and motioned for me to follow him to the door without looking back at the girl. We were almost outside when we heard a voice say:

"My, oh my. If it isn't Paxton Holt!"

We both turned and saw a squat, plump woman come out from the back room behind the counter. She also wore black-framed glasses and had a doughy face. The girl was clearly related to her. Guess this was a family-run business.

"I haven't seen you in a 'coon's age! Good to see you! And—" She looked between the two of us and grinned, waggling her brows. "Glad to see you've moved on. Nasty business. You deserve the best after what happened to—"

"Good to see you too! We'll have to catch up later." Paxton pushed me by the small of my back out the door and it swung shut behind us.

He walked in front of me to the car and I followed in his wake, noticing his shoulders were hiked up and stiff. By the time he had opened the trunk of his car I was beside him. The muscles in his temples were bulging from how tightly he clenched his jaw.

My palms started to sweat in earnest as I felt my anxiety go up another notch. This wasn't like him. I'd seen him angry before, but not like this. I didn't know what to expect so I decided to remain quiet.

He didn't want to talk about what had happened in Marlborough. I would not push him.

He grabbed both of our bags and hauled them out of the car clicking the remote fob on his keys to trigger the trunk to close automatically. I noticed that there was still a briefcase in the trunk but he started walking towards the rooms so again I followed behind him.

We stopped in front of our doors and Paxton put his bag down in front of 116 and mine in front of 117. He started digging in his pockets for the keys, eventually extricating one and using it to open 117 for me.

I put my hand on his arm and he stilled. We stood like that for a few seconds before he turned and looked at me. Several emotions flitted across his face now. Anger, warning, and pain.

I chose my next words carefully. "Thanks for bringing the bags."

He nodded, his shoulders and jaw still tense.

I looked into my room. "Would you... would you like to come in?" I slid my hand from his arm to his shoulder down to his upper waist.

His countenance softened at that. He looked from me to my room. For a moment, I thought he would say yes. He looked as if he wanted to.

But then a cloud passed over his face and he took a step back to face me, breaking contact with my hand as he did so.

"Thanks, but no. I need to freshen up. I can tell I have coffee breath." The corner of his mouth lifted, and I recognized the apology in his humor. He handed me my room key.

"Sure. My tongue feels fuzzy too." I glanced into the room again. "I can see the adjoining door between our suites. I'll leave my side unlocked if you change your mind."

"Sure."

He was halfway through opening his own door before I said, "Paxton?"

"Hmm?"

I raised my arms up. "Can I give you a hug?"

I thought I saw his lower lip quiver before he stepped back and squeezed the breath out of me.

I wrapped my arms around his neck and we stood there for a few moments. I felt my anxiety start to dissipate as his arms pressed into my back. Whatever was bothering him, whatever was going on in his head I wanted him to know that I was there for him. I tried to convey that in my embrace.

Then, without a word, he let go of me and went into his room, shutting the door behind him.

7 MELVIN

Stupid road.

That's what Melvin thought as he drove down it.

Stupid winding road. Stinking late-night shift patrolling the back roads of Marlborough. As if anyone would be out this late, risking their neck or precious Suburban going seventy-five through a forest in the middle of butt-hole nowhere.

He yawned, his eyes threatening to close against the forest brightened by his high-beams. What made this shift worse was being away from his wife and daughter at night.

He just needed the experience. Then they could head back to Colorado where they belonged.

Stupid job.

He let a breath out so that his lips trilled together. On the inhale, he caught a faint whiff of the cleaning product used in the police cruisers and wrinkled his nose.

Stupid smell.

Melvin picked up his travel mug and took a sip only to find that the coffee was almost completely gone.

Great. Stupid. He had ages before he made it to the end of this road, and then he had to head all the way back to Marlborough. He knew he should have stopped at that gas station and topped up on coffee and snacks before he left. Katie had made him a lunch to eat during mid-shift, and he hadn't hesitated to eat it as soon as the first opportunity presented itself. *Stupid.* Now he wished he'd saved it, knowing he'd have the rest of the long shift ahead of him. The ravioli had been cold, but nothing beat Katie's cooking. He put his arm up on the small ledge underneath the car window and rested his head against his fist. As soon as he made it back into town, he was getting the biggest coffee possible and something tasty to munch on for the rest of his shift. Too bad Cobain's wasn't open, or he would go there.

He drove on.

Melvin had his brights on, keeping his eyes open for wildlife. This stretch of road was notorious for deer crossing out of nowhere. Thus far, all he had passed was a dead buck.

Sometime later, Melvin slowed as he came to a T in the road. He looked at the reflective sign. The right arrow pointed towards Seattle and the left arrow pointed towards Marlborough. There was a light pole standing above the sign, but it wasn't on. That was odd.

He squinted.

Was that... was that the back of a head?

Leaning against the light pole, Melvin saw the outline of a small figure. As he sat there, his heart started to beat rather fast for a man who was doing nothing but sitting and staring, the small figure turned, holding up a hand to shield against his headlights.

Hell.

It was a boy.

"Where do you think he came from?" Betsy asked.

Melvin looked at the boy on the other side of the glass, a gray blanket around his shoulders and a bottle of water in his hands. The local doctor was squatting in front of him, looking at a bruise on the boy's leg.

He and the boy had made it back to the Marlborough police station about forty-five minutes ago. It was nearing four in the morning, and Melvin was exhausted but that was nothing on how the boy looked. He was small but had dark wispy hairs at the corners of his mouth, indicating he had at least started puberty. His clothes were old-fashioned, as if they had been handmade in the early 1900s and they were filthy. His pants had mud stains up to his thighs, as if he had walked through a bog. His shirt had rips and holes in them as if a tree had attacked him and he had lost. His face and forearms were covered in scratches and grime.

Most disturbing though, had been the dark brown stains and smears all over the front of his clothes. As if he had held something bloody.

Melvin crossed his arms, shifting his weight from foot to foot. An air vent above the window blew directly onto him and Betsy. Goosebumps formed on his arms like a wave.

"Hell if I know," he replied. "He was just sitting there by that T-stop on the way to Seattle. He looked terrified, his lips all quivering and his body shivering uncontrollably."

Betsy, the Marlborough PD Administrative Assistant, adjusted her large glasses further up her nose. She was a plump and useful sort of woman, her assertive personality demonstrated by her dyed bright red hair and nails.

"Poor boy must have been freezing. No idea how long he'd been out there?" Betsy asked.

"Who knows. By the state of his clothes, at least a day."

"He still hasn't said anything?"

Melvin shook his head. "He didn't say a word to me. Just stared. He teared up when I asked him where his parents were, but otherwise nothing. Took me a while to convince him to get in the cruiser, but he passed out as soon as we started heading back to Marlborough."

"The Doc will be able to help him, surely."

Melvin leaned his weight against the desk, arms still folded tight across his chest. He watched the young Dr. Solomon Compston squatting as he talked to the boy.

"Where's the kid going to go?" Melvin asked, furrowing his brow as he looked at Betsy.

"There's one foster family in town, the Smiths. I've called them, asked if they have room for the boy. Mr. Smith's on his way over now to get him."

Melvin nodded. He liked Jerry Smith. Dependable guy.

"Where could he have come from?" Betsy asked, chewing the end of a manicured nail. "There's nothing out that way for miles and miles."

Melvin shrugged. "I don't know. Circus?"

Betsy smacked his arm with the back of her knuckles. "People don't just join the circus anymore, let alone kids. Don't be dumb."

He had suggested the circus as a means of comic relief, but honestly, he was stumped. There was nothing and no one for miles in any direction up that way. Right?

There was that group of people several miles outside of Marlborough who lived off the land, unplugged from the world. But he had found the boy miles from their compound.

Melvin started as the doctor came out of the room, leaving the boy alone.

"Anything?" Melvin asked. He and Betsy both craned their necks to look into the young doctor's face. He was a giant of a man, towering over them at six-foot-seven.

Solomon shook his head. "His name is Rick. That's all he said."

"Did he indicate anything to you? Where his parents are? How old he is?" Betsy asked.

"No. I'd hazard a guess at thirteen though. Did you call the Smiths?"

"Yes, Jerry is on his way."

Solomon turned around to look at the kid through the glass, his face solemn. Rick had leaned back in the chair so far down that his chest was nearly flush with his thighs.

"But here's what I do know. The kid's covered in blood, right?" Solomon looked back at them over his shoulder. "It's not his."

8 WILLOW

I woke up in a cold sweat, my heart racing. I felt an unfamiliar pillow under my head and a scratchy comforter pressed up against my body.

Where was I? Why wasn't I in my own bed, in my own apartment, safely locked away from the world?

I looked around the dark room, seeing thick curtains pulled over the window with only the smallest amount of warm light peeping through around the edges.

The Glades. I was in a motel. I was in a motel in Marlborough.

Paxton was in the next room over from me.

I took a deep breath, smelling the musty air blowing from the heater under the window, and rubbed my hands over my face.

I was safe.

I picked up my phone and looked at the time. Then I noticed I had a text message from Paxton that had been delivered about twenty-six minutes before.

Morning. Couldn't sleep. Was thinking about heading to Cobain's early. Maybe we can brainstorm. Thoughts?

I texted back right away.

I just woke up. Sure, let's do it.

The message was immediately marked as delivered and read. Three little text dots in a text bubble appeared.

Leave in 30?

I responded.

Sure. Getting ready now.

He sent one more message.

You doing okay? I know it was a new place to sleep last night.

He could have just come in the door and asked me in person. I typed out a short response, not wanting to drag out a text conversation when he was ten feet away from me, merely separated by a wall.

I closed the texting app and opened up the one connected to my home security. I had made sure the camera on my door was on before we had left. It had picked up no movement since we left yesterday afternoon. Paxton's and my apartments were located at the end of our level, so that wasn't too surprising. Still, I felt a sense of relief flow through me. My home was safe. I was safe.

I tossed my phone onto the bed as I sat up and stretched. A manilla folder laid on the pillow next to mine. I had fallen asleep reading it so I flipped the side panel open and pulled out the picture of the carved symbol on Jessie's neck and looked at it again.

I got out of bed and made my way to the bathroom. As I started getting ready for the day, I re-examined the crime scene in my mind's eye.

What was with the partially assembled puzzle? What did that have to do with anything? And why the symbol etched into her skin? What was the connection?

Something about the symbol etched into her skin was sending warning flares up in my mind.

I stepped out into the crisp autumn morning, sliding into my trench coat and wrapping a scarf around my neck. The sky wasn't entirely overcast. Soft yellow light peeped through the evergreens surrounding the hotel.

I took a deep breath. Even despite what lay ahead, it was a beautiful day.

The door beside me opened and Paxton came out of his room. He looked a little better than he had yesterday, likely having gotten a decent night's sleep. He was wearing slacks and a button-up and was in the midst of putting on his light rain jacket when he caught sight of me.

His eyes softened and a smile lined his lips as he said, "Morning sleeping beauty."

The butterflies were back. I returned the smile as I wrapped my scarf around my neck a second time, feeling like I was wearing a neck pillow. "Good morning. How'd you sleep?"

He shrugged as he zipped up his jacket. "Not too bad. You?"

"I never sleep great the first night in a new place."

He nodded, as he pulled his keys out of his pocket. "I wondered. Will a coffee make it better?"

"Coffee makes everything better."

Ten minutes later, we stopped in front of Cobain's and got out. A small gust of the brisk fall air blew into my face, making my eyes water. I looked up at the wooden building full of windows and couldn't help but think that all the glass made it look like a fishbowl.

The idea made me feel exposed.

The bell over the door jingled as we walked in There were a few patrons inside; an older woman was working on a laptop, sipping at what looked like a cappuccino. Two old men wearing veteran baseball hats were chatting in a different corner, sipping on large cups of black coffee. They all looked up and back at the sound of the bell.

Kurtis was cleaning one of the espresso machines as we walked towards the counter. He gave us a nod as he threw the rag onto the counter and met us at the register.

"Morning." He gave a conspicuous look around the shop before whispering "Been keeping an eye out, but I wouldn't hold your breath on him showing up."

"Doesn't look like proximity to the crime scene did any damage to your business," Paxton said as he cast a glance at the patrons.

Kurtis shrugged. "Chief Alvarado kept things pretty hushity-hush for me, bless him."

"That's good. Hate for ol' Cobain's to go down in this mess."

"How's Marie doing?" I asked.

A blush bloomed on Kurtis's face. "I tried to take her home yesterday, but she was a bit of a wreck. Told me she didn't want to be alone so uh... she stayed the night at my place."

Paxton gave an almost imperceptible nod of approval and I smiled openly. "I'm sure she was quite safe."

"Yeah, made it simpler for picking up her car this morning too." He gave us a little conciliatory grin. "Anyways, what can I get started for you? Don't forget, it's discount Tuesday so breves are half off."

Paxton and I proceeded to both order breves and move towards the pickup counter.

While we walked, Paxton turned his attention to me. "I think we should start asking the patrons if they can give us any information about Tony. If they can't, we can go back to the woods and look—"

"Oof!"

Paxton collided with a man who had been walking back from the bathroom.

The man was skinny, his face gaunt and currently annoyed. "Watch it, why don't you?"

"Sorry man," Paxton said.

The man straightened his button-up shirt with a huff. I noticed a little tree stitched on the breast pocket before he walked out of the shop, the bell over the door chiming as he did.

"Looks like coffee didn't do his mood any favors," I said.

"No kidding. I didn't see him at all." Paxton's mouth was down-turned. He looked around the counter to the hall that led to the bathroom, clearly nonplussed.

"Agent? Doctor? Your coffee's ready for you." Kurtis placed two to-go cups on the counter. "Cobain's finest. Hope you enjoy."

"Agent? You all the feds?"

We turned to see the two old men looking at us. One of them was white with a graying mustache that needed a trim. The second man was Black and clean-shaven, rubbing his fingers over his lips.

"Yes." Paxton stood straight, his voice regaining its usual firm confidence. "Can we help you, gentlemen?"

"You here on account of that poor dead girl, no doubt," the second man said. "Heard that young woman was found in the woods nearby."

I cast a swift glance at Kurtis who had picked up the rag from his shoulder and started wiping the counter in the same spot over and over, clearly pretending to be busy.

"We can't discuss details of an active case, Mr..."

"This here is Ted"—The second man pointed with his thumb as he made the introductions—"And I'm Jack."

"Mr. Jack, I'm sure you understand. But—" Paxton cast a furtive look around the shop, as if he was afraid of being overheard. "We do have some questions we're hoping to ask someone. You familiar with Tony?"

Jack raised his eyebrows, glanced at Ted. "I am."

"Would you happen to know where we could find him?"

"There's no knowing where that old bastard might be now, but if you walk up that trail a ways, you'll hit a fork on the path. One way loops back 'round to Marlborough. The other leads to what used to be... private property, shall we say."

"What do you mean by that?" I asked.

"Not too long ago there was this group of folks who lived out in the woods," Jack said. A look of disgust came across his face. "Murderers."

"A group of murderers?" Paxton asked, pulling out his notebook. "How do you know these people committed murder?"

Jack leaned forward, lowering his gravelly voice "Let's just say these folks were strange. They had... dark beliefs. And Tony? Was one of 'em. 'Bout thirteen or fourteen years ago the police were called in to that private property and found... things."

"Did the police arrest anyone?"

"Oh yes," Jack said and Ted nodded.

"He ain't right in the head," Ted said as he picked up his mug and took a large gulp. "Police acquitted him, but we know better."

"So be careful when you find him," Jack said.

Paxton looked up from his notes. "And you think he's still on the property?"

"We walked the trail this morning," Ted said. "We do every Tuesday before coming in for coffee. Saw him hobbling down the fork in the path we mentioned. Wouldn't swear it was him in court though."

"I see." Paxton was scribbling fast. "This is helpful, thank you both."

He took down their information and the old men turned back to their coffee.

"We should go. I want to call the chief." Paxton grabbed his coffee from the counter and led the way out of the shop before I could argue staying for a little longer to see if Tony showed up of his own volition.

I grabbed my cup and waved at Kurtis as I followed Paxton out of the shop.

As I walked to the car, a small knot of anxiety formed in the pit of my stomach. My head was swimming with thoughts of Tony and his connection with the people in the woods.

I had an idea of what the people in the woods were.

I hoped to heaven I was wrong.

9   HOLT

Chief Alvarado said he'd be there in five minutes when I called to explain what we had learned.

Willow walked up to the car while I was on the phone and opened the trunk. She pulled out her spare set of hiking shoes and started putting them on.

I admired the curve of her backside as she bent over to tie the laces before I felt a pang of longing, guilt, and regret shoot through my heart like three separate darts landing the bullseye. I took a deep breath, trying to calm the blood pumping through my neck.

I cleared my throat and leaned against the back bumper. "Chief should be here soon."

Willow looked up at me, still tying one of her boots. Her eyes flickered between the two of mine. She nodded but didn't say anything.

Willow wasn't stupid. She had been quieter than usual since I had snapped at her yesterday. She knew I was holding something back, but I couldn't bring myself to tell her why. To tell her everything. Not yet.

I clenched my jaw, self-loathing slithering into my heart. I was a coward.

Willow finished tying her boots, stood, and dug around the trunk again, eventually pulling out my own hiking boots. She handed them to me and took my coffee.

"Guess what I found out?" she said, a slight quirk to her lips.

"What's that?"

"Cobain's breves are pretty good."

I chuckled in spite of myself.

She slid her hand up my arm to the base of my neck. My heart rate spiked again at her touch, but a second later I could feel my nerves calming. Which, in addition to feeling even more cowardly, had me feeling like I was using her. She didn't deserve this from me.

A police cruiser towing a small forest cart pulled up then. Her hand slid back down my arm as we watched Chief Alvarado and the young mustached officer get out and make their way towards us.

"Holt, Grace. I don't know if you were properly introduced to Deputy Lox yesterday?"

"It's good to see you again," Willow said as he exchanged a nod with each of us.

The chief gestured to the cart. "Borrowed this from the Marlborough Forest Service. Figured I'd save our feet."

Deputy Lox detached it from the cruiser. It had four small seats altogether and could probably only go about forty miles an hour. The rest of us clambered in, the chief in the front next to Lox, with Willow and I in the back. I was very aware of her leg pressing into mine. Her warmth seeped through the cloth of my pants and into my skin. I didn't try to move away from her, even though the guilt came back tenfold.

Lox drove us to the trail entrance and started the trek. It didn't take long for the lush monotony of the forest scenery and the humming of the cart to cause my mind to wander.

The clouds had taken back the sky and obstructed the sliver of sun from earlier so the ambiance of the forest was even gloomier than the day before. It didn't take long for us to pass the crime scene. Police tape still surrounded the small clearing but nothing else was left to indicate that it had been her final resting place. Jessie's body had been removed, and her blood washed away by the on-and-off rain.

We continued down the single path. Other than the drone of the cart, the forest was silent. No wind nor birds made sounds. All that could be heard was the soft patter of the rain that had started falling.

It seemed appropriate to me. As if the forest was giving Jessie a tearful goodbye.

It transported me back in time, to another tragedy not so different from this one. It had also rained the day that—

Nope. Not thinking about that.

I shook my head. My eyes landed on the back of Willow's head as she watched the forest go by. She was in her element here in the woods. I again recalled that this was how she liked to teach her classes at Conifer College, the university she had worked at.

The one she had left because I asked her to.

"Paxton?"

I started. "Huh?"

We had stopped at the fork in the road that Jack and Ted had described. The chief, Deputy Lox, and Willow were all looking at me with expectant expressions indicating they had been talking but I hadn't heard a word of it.

Willow gave me a quick once over as she got out of the cart. "The place the old men were telling us about is up this way, but the trees are too dense for the cart so we're going to have to walk from here. You ready?"

"Yeah, let's get going." I got out of the cart and walked around to Willow's side. The fork in the road wasn't very discernible. The path that looped back to Marlborough was clearly the more used trail, but the other looked less like a path and more like a dear trail.

"Everything okay there, Holt?" The chief walked to my other side and raised a bushy eyebrow at me. "You looked pretty grim for a moment there."

"Everything's fine. It's just... kinda grim out here."

"That it is. Listen, I know how to get to where we're going but I don't know what the place will look like. I don't know what's been taken care of or left over, so... just be prepared." He frowned and started up the path. Deputy Lox followed behind him.

Willow and I exchanged looks.

"I wonder why he's being so enigmatic?" She said.

As we started following, she slid her hand into mine and I felt a semblance of comfort at her touch. I looked over at Willow and saw that cute furrow in her brow, the one that told me she was probably contemplating the same questions I was. What kind of people had lived out this way and what did they believe in? Had they actually committed murder?

We walked in silence for a ways but when I opened my mouth to say something, Willow stopped short.

Her contemplative expression melted away into a look I couldn't read. It was a mixture of grave and recognition. I felt her hand begin to sweat before she pulled away as she walked forward.

I looked around. We were standing at the edge of a clearing. What I had thought were misshapen trees turned out to be small, crumbling single-story wooden structures. The buildings resembled cheap sets used in old western movies, but they were covered in moss and debris from the forest growing around them.

Willow walked up to one of the buildings and touched the wet wood. "These look juvenile almost. As if whoever was in charge built these as a passion project."

"And yet, whole families lived in each one of these." The chief called from the crumbling porch of the next house down. "You guys take a look around. See if you can find Tony or any indication that he might still live here."

Willow and I continued walking, looking at the outside of all the buildings in turn. It seemed to have once been a small settlement.

Willow did a slow spin, taking in everything. "What is this place?"

At the northernmost end of the clearing, about a half football field distance away, was the most dismantled dwelling. Two large trees had been used as the corners of whatever structure had been erected there previously. There was a wall built between the two trees.

Carved deeply into the wood was the symbol from the crime scene. I patted Willow's shoulder and pointed. Her eyes widened and we jogged towards the wall together.

As we got closer, we realized the structure was significantly bigger than the other buildings. The floor was sunken, and at its center stood a tall mound, about five feet high and four feet wide. It had been made from a dark material and covered in leaves and moss. If there had been any other walls, they were long since gone.

I caught a faint whiff of something rotting.

Willow jumped down into the sunken floor and knelt by the mound. "What do you suppose it is?"

I came to her other side and knelt by the mound too. A crunch caused me to look down and I saw the remnants of a disintegrating book under my feet. I toed it, turning the molding cloth biding over, seeing that the pages were all ruined from ages of rain.

"Remains of a book here."

"And here." Willow said, picking up a clump of pages covered in leaves and mildew. "Wonder what they contained?"

I looked back at the mound. My eyes followed a vine that was creeping up the side until the tip of something poking out of the leaves covering the ground caught my eye.

My stomach clenched.

I picked it up, leaves and mulch falling away.

Willow sucked in a soft gasp. "Is that... a femur?"

I stood, my eyes tracing up and down the thing in my hand. Then I looked up at the symbol, like that which we had seen at the crime scene, painted on the wall. "What the hell is this place?"

"Don't be alarmed!"

A few hundred feet away, Deputy Lox raised his hands in a placating way as he took a few slow steps forward. We couldn't see what he was looking at as it was on the other side of a crumbling wooden wall of one of the still partially erect structures. "Mr. Tony? My name is Deputy Lox. We have some questio—"

"Get away from me!"

After a comical *thunk,* Deputy Lox swore at the top of his lungs.

He staggered to the side and a flash of ragged clothing came from behind the wall. A man was hobbling away into another stretch of trees, a crutch under his arm.

I jumped out of the sunken floor and cut him off. "Wait!"

"You get away from me!" The man pulled out a knife from his belt and pointed it at me. I could see the whites of his eyes. Between the leer on his face, the muscles I could see rippling through his holey clothing, and the knife, he was downright frightening to behold.

"Stop right there."

The sound of a bullet entering the chamber echoed through the clearing and everyone stood still.

Chief Alvarado approached, pointing his gun at the man. "Mr. Tony, you are under arrest for assaulting a police officer."

Deputy Lox got to his feet, stumbling as he came forward. Blood ran down his head. His face was etched with fury as he put Tony in handcuffs.

Tony let out a string of swear words.

"If you hadn't hit me, we wouldn't be here," Lox said.

"You scared the shit out of me," Tony snarled. "You can't blame me!"

"All we wanted was to ask you some questions and you attacked me and ran. Now we're bringing you in."

"Lox, get off him." Alvarado came over and helped Tony to his feet, grabbing his crutch. He took a look at Lox's head. "You got a bump, but you'll be alright." The chief looked over at us as Lox and Tony started walking. "Let's go. You guys'll have to ride standing off the back."

"We'll be fine."

I turned back towards Willow. She had hit the dirt when she heard the commotion. I jumped back into the sunken floor and helped her up.

"That's him?" she asked, taking my hand. "He doesn't look like I thought he would."

"Looks every bit as crazy as people have been saying," I said. "Questioning him should be fun."

She turned around and took a few pictures with her phone of the crumbling structure, the mound, and the wall with the faded symbol on it. When she was done, we started walking.

"None of this makes any sense," she said.

"I agree. Especially if that—" I gestured behind me.

"Is what it looks like?"

I noticed that she looked pale. "Are you okay?"

"Paxton, this doesn't just look like a group of weirdos lived here." Willow looked at me, her eyes darting between mine. "This looks like the remains of a blood cult."

10 FIFTEEN YEARS AGO

"HE'S ALWAYS fiddling with that stupid Rubik's cube."

Rick sat on the farthest bench from the school, waiting for his foster mom Laura to pick him up. The woods surrounding the school were starting to change colors. This was one of the first days in months that it had not rained, though the ground around his feet was still wet. The overcast sky was so bright he had to squint when he looked up at it.

He could already tell that he was going to hate high school. The first semester had barely started and everything was just so *hard*.

And the other kids wouldn't leave him alone. A group of sophomores particularly liked to bug him. Even though he had moved as far away from the groups of teenagers waiting for their ride or to board the bus, that group of sophomores had followed him.

Yet again.

They surrounded the bench and the leader, a tall kid named Jaz, grabbed the cube from Rick's hands.

Rick made to grab it back, but two of the kids behind him grabbed his shoulders and pulled him back onto the bench.

Jaz started twisting the cube up. Rick felt a surge of annoyance—he had been almost done solving it. Rubik's cubes were his current obsession. He was trying to master the formula of solving the puzzle by memory.

"Aww, did I mess up your widdle toy?" Jaz adopted a mock baby voice. "Is da widdle freshy sad? Whatcha gonna do about it?"

Rick said nothing. He just glared at the ground.

"So pathetic. He never talks, never looks anyone in the eye, and is always messing with something in his hands. Bet he's autistic." Jaz threw the Rubik's cube on the ground and stomped on it.

Rick winced when he heard the plastic crack and then gasped as he was pushed off the bench to the ground, landing on all fours at Jaz's feet.

"Hey!"

Everyone looked around at the unexpected voice. A girl, one of the seniors, was walking over.

"Oh hey," Jaz said, an embarrassed smile forming on his lips as he pushed his hand through his hair. "What's up—"

"What's your problem? He wasn't doing anything. He was just minding his own business and you guys start harassing him?" The girl's eyes were flashing with anger. "Jason Snider, so help me if you keep this up, I'll quit being your tutor. It's only because of me that you passed any of your classes last semester, otherwise you'd have been held back a year. This is your last chance. Quit being an asshole."

Jaz's whole face flushed. He looked angry but the teeniest bit of shame colored his cheeks.

"As for the rest of you—" the girl waved her hands at the other boys— "Beat it."

The boys shuffled around, waiting to see what Jaz would do. He looked down at Rick.

"Prick," he muttered and walked away.

One by one, the rest of the group left.

She shook her head and huffed before turning back to Rick. Her expression softened as she offered him her hand.

He took it and used it for balance as he stood. Her arms were long and graceful. She was a little bit taller than him too.

"You okay?" she asked.

Rick looked down at the broken Rubik's cube at their feet. He bent back down and started picking the pieces up.

"I like Rubik's cubes too." The girl bent down beside him and offered her hand again so he could put the pieces into her open palm. "I like all kinds of puzzles actually. What about you?"

Rick looked up at her. She had the most captivating cobalt blue eyes. Her dark hair rested on her shoulders, creating pretty loops of brown and copper.

She was beautiful.

He looked down. He nodded.

They finished picking up the pieces and together threw the broken puzzle into the trash by the bench.

Just then, Laura's car pulled up. She waved at Rick, smiling.

"Well, see ya." The girl smiled at him and walked away.

He blinked. She had such a pretty smile.

He turned and got into Laura's car.

"Did I see you throwing away your Rubik's cube?" his foster mom asked. Laura was nice but had the tendency to be impatient.

Rick nodded.

Laura clicked her tongue. "Why? I just got that for you."

Rick shrugged, keeping his eyes on the road in front of them.

"Were those boys picking on you again today?"

Rick didn't say anything.

"I'm sorry, honey. Who's the girl, though? She's pretty."

Rick shrugged again.

"I wonder if that's the Larrisons' youngest daughter. She certainly looked like it. Her mom goes to my book club."

Rick cast a glance at Laura out of the corner of his eye before looking back at the road.

"Alright, alright! Gosh, so chatty today."

Rick lips turned up in a reluctant grin.

11 WILLOW

I FELT for the poor man on the other side of the glass.

We were all back at the Marlborough PD. Lox and the chief brought Tony into an interrogation room while Paxton and I moved into the observation room on the other side of the one-way mirror window.

I leaned my body weight forward on my hands, resting against the table under the window. I'd been inside interrogation rooms before, and it brought me no pleasure to see one again, even from this side of the glass.

The room they'd put Tony in was entirely light gray. Even the table and chairs were colorless. The florescent light cast a harsh shadow over Tony's face.

He looked so haggard. His dark hair and beard were peppered with gray and in desperate need of a wash and trim. His clothes were worn and holey.

I had watched him walk between the chief and Lox when we made our way back from that place in the woods. He had walked with a severe limp, as if one of his legs were shorter than the other, but he still stood over six feet.

He was formidable, and his ragged appearance only made him more frightening.

His wrists were bound in handcuffs and he rocked back and forth in his seat, not looking at anything in particular. He hadn't spoken since getting arrested, but I had seen him move his lips a few times.

Tony was exercising his right to remain silent, it appeared.

The observation room was dark and muted due to the cloth walls. There were a couple of desks and chairs in the room, along with recording equipment.

Paxton was standing on my right, jotting some notes down in his notepad, scuffing the heel of his right foot against the ground as he wrote.

I also shifted my weight. My hands felt sweaty, and my thoughts whirled around my head like water down a drain.

Paxton had pulled up a femur from the base of that altar.

Yes, *altar*. And *femur*.

Why was there an altar? Who were these people in the woods? In all my studies, I had never heard of a blood cult in this area of Washington.

Chief Alvarado walked into the room, holding a file.

Paxton rolled his shoulders back, closing his notebook and crossing his arms. "Chief, we gotta talk."

I stood up and turned towards the chief too.

"We're going in blind here. Nothing is making sense. We have this home- less man that everyone is leery of, we have the remains of what looked like an entire settlement in the woods that there are whispers of it being the home of a group of murders. Before Deputy Lox caught Tony, Willow and I found what looked to be a *human femur* at the base of what I'm now positive was an altar under a wall that had an engraving in the same shape as the marking around Jessie's stab wound. To top it all, nearly everyone seems to think that man in there has something to do with all of it."

Paxton glanced at me and I nodded. "Be honest with us. There was a blood cult that was living in the woods outside of Marlborough, wasn't there?"

The chief sighed. He leaned against the table, taking his hat off and rubbing his fingers through his hair.

"You're right. It was a few years before I worked for Marlborough PD, so I wasn't there for any of this. A buddy of mine, Melvin Klein, was. He told me everyone knew some people lived off the land not far outside of Marlborough. Not terribly uncommon. They kept to themselves—we didn't bother them, they didn't bother us.

"Until hikers started disappearing. There was no connection of any kind found between the disappearances and the group of people, so they were never investigated until the PD got an anonymous call that something sinister was happening out at the compound. Shortly after, the PD got a call from some people using the trail to come out to the woods because shouts and screams had been heard. Melvin was one of the deputies that went out to the site. What he told me they saw…"

I felt my palms start to sweat again in earnest when I witnessed the grizzly bear of a chief go pale.

"It was diabolical. A pile of bodies in the clearing, all bloody and mangled. Men, women, and… and children."

My stomach clenched. I kept my eyes on the chief, but sensed Paxton lean against the table beside me. He very briefly touched his hand to my lower back. I was grateful for how dark the room was.

"He told me almost everyone was dead. There were only a couple of people in robes running around when they got there, but they were quickly apprehended and taken in for questioning. From what they could gather in their interrogations, those people in the woods were, as you said, part of a blood cult, trying to resurrect a lost deity by making sacrifices of dismembered body parts. That was where the hikers had gone. It sounded like someone within the compound, one of the hikers, got hold of a cellphone and called the police out. When the robed ones discovered that… it became a bloodbath. 'The Bloodless One's rage is enacted by the Limbless Ones' on the flock,' was repeated over and over."

The chief gestured at the window with the file. "He was one of the robed ones."

Paxton's look of shock reflected how I felt. We both looked at Tony who was still sitting and rocking in his chair.

"So why isn't he in jail?" Paxton asked.

"From what I was told, there was not a single drop of blood on his robes. All the others were drenched. Because of that, there was no way to prove he did anything. Secondly, he wasn't chanting anything about the Bloodless One or Limbless Ones. Just kept silent."

The chief stood. "Between the three of us, I don't know if he killed Jessie. But I do think he might be able to point us in the right direction."

"We need to talk to him," Paxton said.

"With your area of expertise, I agree. Maybe he'll respond better to you two."

"Look," I said.

Paxton and the chief followed my line of sight to Tony. He had stopped rocking and was looking at the window. The crazed look in his eye had dissipated, replaced by unnerving intensity.

As if he could see us through the window.

Alvarado opened the observation room door for us and ushered us out. He handed Paxton the file he had been holding and opened the next door over. "Pictures of Jessie. Good luck. I'll be watching."

Tony looked up and watched us as Paxton and I entered the room. His gaze was intense and focused. I noticed his eyes were the palest of greens.

We sat. I did a quick scan of the room and held in a shudder. The air was still, but the room felt cold. Goosebumps erupted on my arms.

Tony removed his hands from the table and sat back, never taking his eyes off us. "You're the feds."

I rubbed my sweaty hands on my thighs. His voice was coarse, only from lack of use. He held himself with an air of competence and assuredness, as if he was used to commanding whatever room he was in. The look in his eye was piercing, as if he was scrutinizing everything about us. He didn't strike me as even a little bit crazy.

And that scared me. Perhaps he was the type of crazy that knew how to mask.

"Why are you content to let the townsfolk think you're a monster?" Paxton asked.

Tony turned his pale eyes to Paxton, his eyebrows raised in what appeared to be genuine surprise. "What?"

I also was a little bit startled. This wasn't the approach I would have gone with, but I was interested to see Paxton's angle.

Paxton put his hands on the table and folded them together. "You heard me."

Tony narrowed his eyes at Paxton but didn't say anything.

"The reason I ask," Paxton said, "Is because most people, whether upstanding citizens or complete psychos, care about their reputation. No one *wants* to be considered a monster. But you seem to have done nothing to try and change people's minds. Why?"

Tony continued to gaze at Paxton. I noticed his chest was starting to rise and fall the tiniest bit faster, as if his heart rate had accelerated.

"We have some questions regarding a young woman." Paxton opened the folder, resting it against the table at an angle so Tony couldn't see the file's contents. Inside were several pictures of Jessie, all when she was still alive and well. Paxton picked a picture and slid it towards Tony, closing the file at the same time. "Do you recognize her?"

Tony looked at the picture in silence. He took a deep breath and opened his mouth.

The door banged open, causing all of us to jump.

The chief caught the door as it bounced off the wall. His eyes bore into me and Paxton. "A word. *Now*." He held the door open for us as Paxton and I stood and hurried through it.

I turned as the door shut behind us. Tony held my gaze until the door closed.

"Chief, what is it?" Paxton's brows were furrowed.

"Another body was found."

12 FOURTEEN YEARS AGO

Rick sat on her living room floor, pretending to be absorbed in the pieces in from of him, but really he was looking at her as she bustled about the kitchen, putting cookies and glasses of milk on a tray.

She had come up to him after second period one day after they had met and said without any preamble, "Hey, I got this new puzzle that I wanted to start working on this afternoon. Would you like to come over and work on it with me?"

It wasn't until she'd said, "Hello? Anyone in there?" that he'd realized that he had been standing there, staring at her with his mouth agape in surprise.

Surely, *surely*, he must have been mistaken. There was no way the pretty girl that had stood up for him was inviting him over to her house.

"Is that a no or what?" she had asked, the corner of her mouth turning up.

Nope, she had really meant it.

He'd smiled at her and nodded, his bag falling off his shoulder with the exuberance of his affirmation.

"Cool. I'll meet you by the bleachers after school's out. I can give you a ride." She'd given him that pretty smile and left, her dark curls flicking behind her as she turned and walked away.

Wow. *Wow.*

He'd had a hard time paying attention in class for the rest of the day and had nearly tripped over his feet as he had made his way to the bleachers after the last bell rang. He'd sent Laura a text letting her know where he was going to be for the afternoon. She had responded instantly.

Oh good! The Larrisons are nice. I hope you have a good time.

They had been doing puzzles together a couple times a week ever since.

She brought the tray into the living room and put it to the side so it wasn't in the way of the puzzle on the coffee table. They were about half-way done with the 1000-piece puzzle. As Rick grabbed a cookie, her phone buzzed. She picked it up and her eyes went wide as she said, "Holy shit."

Startled, he turned his head towards her so fast his neck cricked. He rubbed his palm against it, trying to get the ache to subside as he watched her turn the TV to the local news channel.

MARLBOROUGH BREAKING NEWS flashed at the bottom of the screen in bold red. A newscaster in a tan raincoat stood at one of local trail entrances.

"... just in. Police received a call from an anonymous source about a commotion in the woods a few miles outside of Marlborough. The police were sent to investigate and discovered a pile of mutilated human bodies in the center of a private compound. It is unknown who caused such a violent scene, but several suspects were apprehended."

"That's horrible," she said, her fingers covering her mouth. "Those poor people."

Rick felt his stomach writhe. The cookie went from sweet to sand in his mouth. It took all his will power to not hurl all over the coffee table.

The camera flashed from the reporter to a grainy long-distance shot of police officers pushing several people in handcuffs into the back of some police cruisers.

"To think something like that could have happened, right in our back-yard." She shook her head and turned to look at him. "Rick? Are you okay?"

He tightened his jaw, feeling as if he might throw up if he opened it.

"Rick?"

He started taking deep breaths, trying to calm his nerves but the smell of copper was invading his nose.

"Rick, talk to me." She scooched closer to him. "What's going on?"

He rocked back and forth, trying to make the dizziness stop. He forced himself to keep taking deep breaths.

She glanced between him and the TV before turning it off. She put her hand on his shoulder, and instantly his mind was put at ease. Everything stopped spinning and his stomach stopped churning.

"I never realized... we were so close to Marlborough." He tore his eyes from the screen to her face. He raised his eyebrows ever so slightly.

"You mean...wait." Her eyes furrowed in confusion before the smallest inkling of comprehension flashed across her face. "Do you—"

Her phone rang. She answered it, still leaving her other hand on his shoulder.

Her touch was so soothing. He watched her while she talked, not taking in a word of her conversation. All his attention was on her beautiful features and her hand on his shoulder. He blinked when she turned to look at him, putting her phone down on the coffee table. He was startled by how close they were sitting.

"My older sister Callie and my niece are gonna be over later for dinner. Would... would you like to stay, or do you want me to give you a ride home?" Her eyes were filled with concern. He hadn't been looked at with that kind of warmth since—

He blinked again. "I'd... I'd like to stay."

She nodded, her expression still full of warmth and kindness, but he could see that her brow was still furrowed. Then she did something she had never done before.

She mussed up his hair.

Then she picked up the plate and stood.

"I'm going to get us some more cookies. I'll be right back." She walked towards the kitchen.

Rick felt chills over his whole body. Her touching him felt *right*.

Wherever she was, he needed to be.

13 WILLOW

AFTER WE HAD WATCHED the officers take pictures of the crime scene, the coroner Sinsae Jones, a small Indian woman, started examining the body.

We were in the woods again but on a different trail. The trees were a little denser here, casting everything in shadow. The ground was filled with slick mud and everyone's shoes were covered in a thick layer of muck. The victim was damp with rain. She hadn't been out here long enough to have gotten drenched. Paxton, Chief Alvarado and I watched from a little distance so as to not crowd the coroner. Even from this distance, I could see the victim's makeup was running from the water pooling in the indents of her eyes.

"Who called this in?" Paxton asked. His arms were crossed with his notepad tucked under his arm, his pen acting as a bookmark.

"Some teenagers. Deputy Lox has already talked to them. Apparently they were all higher than kites and panicked when they found her. Had a hard time getting anything coherent out of them," Chief Alvarado replied.

"It takes a toll on you, discovering a body." Paxton murmured.

I had my hands buried in my coat pockets. "Especially under the influence. But this can't have been Tony, can it?"

Alvarado rubbed the back of his neck. "It'll depend on what Sinsae says about time of death, but it seems highly unlikely. He's been at the PD since this morning. Plus, we're miles away from where we picked him up. And he's got a limp."

"Chief!" Sinsae waved us all over.

We approached the coroner and I got my first good look at the body.

She looked as if she were just sleeping, just taking a nap in the soft mud and sprinkling rain.

She was laying on her back, her head tiled to the side, eyes closed. She wore high-end hiking clothes that, aside from all the blood, were pristine, as if she had just bought them. Her dark, coppery hair was fanned out from her head, one side looking like a princess. The other side was darkened with half-dried blood from the wound in her neck. The same puzzle piece symbol was carved around the stab wound.

My eyes trailed down her body and I felt the back of my throat tighten when I noticed her missing limbs. The scene was too similar to the one from yesterday. When we got to this one, my brain must have filled in the missing gaps to delay the shock. But standing here, my brain couldn't protect me from the horror of seeing another dismembered body.

Both of her arms were missing, entirely hacked off at the shoulder. The blood from her wounds had soaked into the mulch under her, leaving the dark ground a stark contrast with her blanched skin.

On top of her chest was another partially completed piece of a puzzle, just like the other victim. It was a different corner this time, but the image was just as hard to discern. It was dark blue along the edge with a red patterned bar underneath.

Sinsae stood, looking between Paxton and me.

"Sinsae, meet FBI Agent Holt and Dr. Grace. Holt, Grace, this is Sinsae Jones, our coroner." Chief said.

Sinsae nodded at us. "Pleasure. I'd shake your hands..." She wiggled her latex clad fingers which were covered in blood before looking down at the body. "I'm told an ID was found on her, Issie Gordon. Died from blood loss induced from the severed upper limbs and punctured jugular." She pointed to the wound on Issie's neck. "Same symbol carved into the skin as the previous victim."

"Estimated time of death?" The chief asked.

"I'd estimate sometime between ten this morning and noon. But with the rain, it's hard to know for sure."

I looked up at Paxton, expecting to exchange a glance, but he wasn't looking back at me. His brows were furrowed. He had started taking notes as soon as we approached the body, but now he was twiddling the pen between his index and middle finger against his leg again, leaving ink marks on his pants. His gaze was fixed so hard on the body, it was like he was trying to see through her, as though her corpse could tell him who had done this to her.

"I'm thinking this wasn't Tony," I said, looking between him and the chief.

"Agreed. It can't have been Tony," Alvarado replied.

I turned to Paxton again and saw his look of agitation deepen. His eyes had not once left the body. I'm not sure he'd even blinked. He ran a hand through his hair, causing it to stand on end.

"Paxton?" I looked around, trying to be discreet. "Are you okay?"

He started. "Huh?" He looked at me and seemed surprised to see me standing there. "What? I'm fine, just... damn." He rubbed his hand over his face.

Sinsae gave Holt an understanding look. "Seeing someone dismembered would turn anyone's stomach."

"It's not that it's just... I feel like I've seen that puzzle piece before."

I looked back at the corner of the puzzle on her chest. "I'm going to guess they go together. Do you know what picture it makes? Because I can't tell."

Paxton shook his head. "I have no idea."

14 THIRTEEN YEARS AGO

RICK HAD NOT WANTED to go to this stupid party.

He didn't want to see her again.

That was a lie. He wanted nothing *but* to see her again. But this was her goodbye party before she went off to college. Before she went off and left Marlborough.

Before she went off and left him.

So he sat outside on the cushioned love-seat swing, listening to everyone else laughing through the open window. The light breeze blew against his face, carrying a smell of rain, BBQ, and grass.

Her older sister and brother-in-law were there. Her niece was running around, making a racket. All her family and friends were there, joking around and having a good time. It was almost like they were happy she was going.

He knew better than all those morons in there. College meant she was leaving for good. Sure, she would *probably* come back, but she wouldn't be the same. She would be older, different. Not *his*.

Not the same.

He hated that. He just wanted her to stay here forever. He was going to ask her tonight. He had to. His very *being* depended on her staying. He couldn't risk losing her anymore than he already was.

She would say no at first. She didn't know how he felt about her. But he would convince her. Somehow.

He looked over at the living room window, to the shelf in the corner. It was full of the puzzles the two of them had spent hours putting together over the past year.

She hadn't gotten rid of a single one. That almost made him smile.

The door flew open.

"Rick!" She came over to him and sat down beside him on the swing, flopping back and letting her feet swing up off the ground. "There you are. Why are you out here all by yourself?"

He shrugged, burying his hands further into his pockets.

"Why so glum, chum? There'll be cake later." She threw her arm around his shoulder as she whisper-sang in his ear, "I asked for reeeed velveeet."

That did make him smile. He loved red velvet.

"I have something for you."

She put a small, wrapped package on his lap.

He picked it up, raising an eyebrow at her. "Isn't it customary for the person leaving to be the one receiving gifts?"

"I don't see anything behind *your* back," she said in a mocking voice. She pushed his shoulder, gesturing at the present.

He opened it. Under the wrapping was a puzzle.

"I've already solved this one. It's one of my favorites, so I wanted you to have it."

Rick felt warmth spread all the way from his heart to his toes.

"Let's get a picture together!" She pulled one of the lawn chairs over and placed her phone on top. She dashed back and sat right next to him, throwing an arm around his shoulders. She picked up the puzzle box with the other. "Grab it and smile!"

He did, forcing himself to smile. He looked over at her and saw her beautiful mouth curved upward, exposing her teeth. That made it easier for him to soften into the uncomfortable expression.

She jumped back up and grabbed her phone from the chair. "Perfect. I had it take a picture cluster, so we'll have options." She grinned at him again and plopped back down beside him. She looked out at the yard. Taking a deep breath. "Man, I'll miss this place."

And his happy bubble popped. "Do you have to go?"

"Of course I have to go. I'm excited for it. It's my next big adventure."

"I wish you weren't going. I-I want you to stay."

She looked at him, puzzled. "I'll be back. It's not like you'll never see me again."

"Won't be the same."

"I'll still be the same me I've always been. Just more educated. And poorer." She blew a short raspberry.

Now was the time to do it. To tell her that she had to stay. For him. Because he needed her.

He opened his mouth and—

Her phone dinged.

She pulled it out, and a goofy smile, one that he had never seen before, lit up her face. Her thumbs flew over the screen.

"I was going to tell you—I actually already have a friend there," she said as she closed her phone. Her cheeks were pink.

Rick raised his eyebrows, confused. Why did she look like that?

"Yeah. When I toured the campus, I... well... I met this guy. His name's Ax. We hit it off and exchanged numbers."

A writhing knot formed in Rick's stomach.

"He's a sweet guy. I'm excited to see him again." Her phone dinged again and her goofy grin got bigger, her cheeks more pink.

The back door opened and one of her friends waved and yelled, "Cake time!"

She lightly smacked Rick's shoulder with the back of her hand. "Let's go!"

"Wait, there's something... I do have something to give you." If he didn't do it now, he would lose her forever.

She gave him a quizzical look, tilting her head to the side. "What is it?"

His heart began to pound. "Well, uh. It's not behind my back. But you have to close your eyes."

She narrowed her beautiful cobalt eyes at him, but she never stopped grinning. She closed them and he admired her long lashes. Her face was gorgeous as she waited for him to give her what he'd been longing to since the moment they'd met.

He had never done this before. He had watched other people do it and it didn't look that hard. She wouldn't listen to words so maybe—

"Ugh!" She pushed him away, spitting and wiping her mouth. "What the hell, Rick?"

"Wait, I'm trying to—"

"No!" She jumped up. "That was hugely inappropriate. Don't *ever* do that again." She gave him a disgusted look, the same look she had given Jaz all those months ago, before turning on her heel and going back into the house.

Numb. His whole body became numb as shame engulfed him.

That had gone far worse than he imagined. She clearly didn't understand what he had been trying to do.

She avoided him the rest of the evening.

She hadn't even left and she was already long gone.

15 WILLOW

Sinsae told us Dr. Solomon would contact us first thing the next morning. Paxton and I remained at the crime scene long enough to also interview the teenagers who had found Issie, but we got nothing more out of them than Lox had.

By then, it had been late evening and Alvarado sent us home. Neither of us argued and headed back to the motel. I had kept an eye on Paxton but he had regained his usual confident demeanor after that moment earlier. As we drove, we made plans to meet in the morning for coffee, but I could tell his mind was somewhere else. We pulled into the motel and stepped out of the car in silence.

At our room doors, he said goodnight to me without another word. No kiss on the cheek, not even a smile. I got into bed that night wondering where his mind was and why he wouldn't talk to me about it.

"We still need to finish that interview with Tony," I said the next morning as we pulled into Cobain's. I had slept much better than the previous night and it looked like Paxton had too. The circles under his eyes weren't quite so pronounced.

"I know. I'm thinking we go to the M.E.'s office and see what we discover. And then we'll go back to Tony. He's not going anywhere for the time being." Paxton unbuckled his seatbelt.

"Sounds good to me."

We got out and walked towards the building. The fishbowl structure was now becoming familiar and that helped soothe the anxiety of being in a new place.

Paxton held the door open for me as we went inside. A young couple were sitting across from each other at one of the tables, one with what looked like a refresher in front of them and the other with an iced coffee. Judging by how nervous they both looked, I guessed they were on a first date.

An older man, with round glasses perched on the tip of his nose was sitting in a corner, reading a newspaper, a half empty mug on the table beside him.

Then there was a young woman, likely in her mid-twenties, sitting in the farthest corner. Her head was in her hand as she looked down at a book splayed open on the table in front of her. Her other hand was wrapped around an untouched latte beside the book. It appeared to be a library book because I could see the plastic casing around the cover. Her dark hair fell in front of her face, shielding it from the rest of the shop.

Kurtis was restocking the to-go cups as we walked towards the counter. When he saw us, he gave us a nod as he finished his task and met us at the cash register.

"How's it going?" He asked, leaning against the counter.

"No rest for the weary. And nothing but rest for the dead," Paxton said.

Kurtis raised an eyebrow and bit his lip, looking contemplative. "Makes sense to me."

"Marie still doing okay?" I asked.

Kurtis grinned. "Yes ma'am, she's doing much better. What about you guys? Heard things are uh... still unsolved?"

Paxton gave him a tight-lipped shrug and I nodded.

He raised his hands. "I know, can't talk about an ongoing investigation. I'll just hope you guys keep coming back so I can keep supplying you with ample caffeine until it's solved. Now, what can I get you?"

"That mocha breve you made for me yesterday was delicious," I said. "I'll have another one of those."

Paxton looked at the menu, his brow furrowed. "I don't know what I want. What would you suggest?"

Kurtis nodded towards the young woman. "She ordered a hazelnut mocha latte. Never had anyone order that before, but it sounded tasty. Basically Nutella and coffee in a liquid form."

Paxton glanced back and froze.

I turned in the direction he was looking and saw the young woman. She had sat up and pulled her dark hair to the side, revealing a lovely face. She let out an audible gasp at whatever she was reading. The movement seemed to have brought her back to reality a little because she did a small double take at her latte as if she had forgotten it was there. She took three big gulps and placed the cup down with a loud clatter in the saucer. She made an "oops" face and glanced around the shop, stopping when she caught sight of Paxton staring at her.

They held each other's gaze for a solid five seconds before Paxton ducked his head and looked away. He had gone white.

"Paxton?" I reached out to him, but he moved away.

He glanced back at the young woman. She also had gone pale. She shoved the cup and saucer away from her, dark liquid sloshing down the sides of the mug. She stood, her whole face pink now as she grabbed her coat, bag, and book. She gave Paxton another look and me a quick glance before ducking through the doors.

Paxton turned back quickly to Kurtis who was looking slightly nonplussed. "That woman, who just left? What was her name?"

Kurtis glanced at the door. "Her? That's Del. Delphi Augur."

Paxton leaned against the counter.

I noticed his forehead and upper lip had a slight sheen of sweat. I tentatively touched his forearm, Kurtis and I exchanging a look of concern.

"Paxton?" I asked, rubbing his arm.

Paxton stood there for a few seconds, his eyes unfocused. Then he blinked, cleared his throat, and stood up straight. "I'll take a hot hazelnut mocha latte."

"Uh...You got it, man." Kurtis cast one more glance at me as he started marking the side of the to-go cup.

"Thanks." Paxton walked to the end of the counter. I paid for the drinks and then followed.

"What was that about?" I asked him, my concern making my voice come out more aggressive than I had intended.

"What was what about?"

"Don't give me that." I crossed my arms. "You know I'm talking about that girl that just left. That girl you were *gawking* at, by the way."

Paxton looked away.

"Did you know her?"

"I... I thought I recognized her."

I stepped up to him and ran my hand up and down his arm, in the same way I would if I was trying to warm him up. "You're scaring me a little. I just want to know what's going on in your head. You haven't been yourself since we got to Marlborough."

He put his hand over mine. "I know. I'm sorry. It's just... hard for me to talk about."

The sound of cups hitting the counter caused us both to look around. Kurtis looked between us, a look of concern still on his face. "Here are those drinks for ya."

"Thanks Kurtis."

"You guys take it easy," he said, raising his eyebrows at me before moving away.

Paxton looked down at his pocket and pulled out his phone. An incoming message alert vibrated in his hand. He grimaced. "It's the chief. Said Dr. Solomon found something and he wants us to go over to check it out and report."

"Did he say what it was?"

"No." Paxton took a drink of his coffee and started walking to the door. "Only one way to find out."

I grabbed my cup and waved at Kurtis as I followed Paxton out of the shop. I took a drink of my breve, my head swimming. Bodies, Tony, the blood cult, and...

And the way Paxton had looked at that young woman.

As if he had seen a ghost.

16   WILLOW

PAXTON and I had left the coffee shop and headed directly to the medical examiner's office. I had insisted on driving. Paxton seemed mostly recovered from whatever had come over him in Cobain's, but his face was still bloodless.

He was too distracted to argue with me which only further proved to me that he was hiding something. He'd dissociated more times than I could count in just the last few days. The way he'd looked when he came into town. The way he'd looked at that girl. I'd felt something was wrong the moment we got here, but now I *knew* something was wrong. And I was starting to worry about whether he could handle this case.

I don't want to do this without him.

The ME's office was a square brick building, clearly new. The parking lot had freshly painted lines and the landscaping had the manicured look that only expensive or new establishments had.

We pulled in and got out of the car. I looked over at Paxton and raised my eyebrows at him which he only acknowledged with a small nod before we started walking. He didn't look at me again as we walked to the entrance in silence.

The interior of the building consisted of a small, brightly lit lobby with a singular hallway. The décor was sparce. The only color was that of the green laminate flooring. There were several windows, all looking out onto trees.

"Hello there. You must be Agent Paxton Holt and Dr. Willow Grace?"

I looked back at the hallway. Emerging from around the corner was the tallest man I had ever seen. If I had stood on my toes and tried to touch the crown of his amber head, I wouldn't have been able to. He was easily past six-foot-five, but rather than being intimidating, he had a kind smile partially obscured by a bushy beard and even kinder brown eyes.

"That's us." I said.

"Pleasure to meet you. I'm Dr. Compston but please, call me Solomon. I'm the Marlborough ME," he said, shaking both of our hands. "Chief Alvarado told me the two of you were coming. Hope you didn't have too much to eat before coming here. Being in the showroom can be a... disquieting experience."

"Just coffee," Paxton said. His complexion had started to return to normal. The way he addressed the ME and how he held himself was in his usual manner— composed and controlled.

Solomon let out a loud, booming bark of a laugh. The sound of it could melt ice, it was so infectious. "Coffee and corpses! Delightful combination. One of my favorites."

Even Paxton had started grinning.

"Let me show you 'round." Solomon gestured for us to follow him down the hall. He spoke as he walked and pointed to different doors. "That door leads to the offices. That door leads to the file room. And this door leads to the showroom."

"Rather a macabre name for where you dissect bodies," I said, as he scanned his key card against the machine by the door.

He pushed the door open and walked into the room, holding it open for us. "There's gotta be something humorous in this line of work." The side of his mouth lifted. "Obviously aside from the humerus bone."

Paxton snorted as he followed the doctor inside.

As soon as I entered the room, the immediate ambient temperature dropped. The smell was a mix of cold air, sterile cleaning chemicals, and formaldehyde. The overwhelming smell I tried not to focus on was that of the corpse covered in a sheet on the table in the center of the room. I only barely stifled my gag. Paxton was also looking at the corpse, a slight crinkle to his nose.

The whole place was white and sterile. Even the overhead fluorescent lights were almost too bright to bear. Across the room was a wall lined with body lockers. Only a handful were tagged, and were probably the only ones in use. Only a handful of known corpses in Marlborough.

I turned my attention back to the table in the center of the room. Issie's body lay there, all but her head and neck covered in a white sheet.

"I have already done a preliminary examination of both bodies." Solomon adjusted his glasses further up his nose as he walked around the table. He pulled a pair of gloves out of a dispenser on the wall by a sanitation station and snapped them on. He looked over his glasses at both of us. "And I found something I'd like to show you. However, be warned. Even cleaned, the wounds are egregious. Please feel free to step out if you need to."

My stomach started to fill with what felt like writhing worms.

He pulled the sheet down further, resting the edge across her shoulder. Issie's face and neck were much cleaner now than they had been the last time I had seen her. She almost looked normal, barring the stab wound surrounded by the etched symbol in the flesh of her neck.

He pulled the sheet down to her chest, giving us a clear view of two stumps. All that remained of her arms. Even cleaned, they were ghastly to look at. We could see the hollow in the flesh where the shoulder socket was supposed to be.

"This is what I wanted to show you." He pointed to the left stump. "It looks like her arm has been sawed off."

Paxton cleared his throat. "We uh... ascertained as much."

"No, really look at it. Her arm wasn't removed by someone in a frenzy." Solomon narrowed his eyes. "The flesh would be jagged and mutilated. That's not the case here."

"What are you suggesting then?" I asked.

"Her arm was removed by someone who knew what they were doing. It's the same level of precision on Jessie, missing her legs. Knowing this might help narrow down who's responsible for this. But...I've seen this before."

Paxton and I exchanged glances as he pulled out his notepad, "When? How?"

Solomon stood and leaned against the table, looking at us over his glasses. "I know they took you to the remains of the place in the woods near Cobain's. It operated about fourteen or fifteen years ago."

"The blood cult," I said.

He nodded. "I examined the bodies from that case too. Some had their limbs hacked off, while others had theirs removed surgically."

"Did anything else about the bodies stand out to you?" Paxton's pen hovered over his notepad.

"About a handful of the bodies found were not a part of the cult, but rather were hikers that had been reported missing. It was naturally somewhat of a relief when they were discovered. Solved almost all the missing person cases open at the time. Only one person was never found."

"Do you remember who?" I asked.

Solomon scrunched his forehead as he looked down. "The guy was a doctor of some kind, I think. I want to say his name was Antonio Vermont."

Something clicked in my head. I looked over at Paxton, feeling my face get warm despite the coolness of the room. "Tony."

He furrowed his brows at me.

I turned back to the doctor, feeling breathless. "Do you still have those case files?"

17 TEN YEARS AGO

It was perfect.

I watched the movers bring our stuff into the house from our front lawn. *Our* house, *our* front lawn. It was hard not to start singing at the top of my lungs. I was so happy. Happier than I had ever been. Even the damp, drizzly, dark weather couldn't put a dampener on my spirits.

I had graduated from college, met a great guy, gotten married, and now we were starting our lives together. I was so grateful to get a job working for Marlborough. I wanted to give back to my community in every way I could while Ax went through his training.

People had said we got married really fast. They thought we rushed into it. But so what? I knew from the moment I'd met him that he was going to be there until the day I died. But I wasn't *quite* ready to leave home. Not permanently.

The front of our house faced the woods. There was a sidewalk running parallel to the forest front. Perfect for morning jogs and walks with the puppy I was going to convince Ax to get us.

As I directed the movers where to place some crates, I walked towards our mailbox. I knew nothing would be inside of it, but I wanted to look anyways. Perhaps there would some coupons—I knew the post office often gave coupons to people who had just moved.

I put my hand on the mailbox, but before I could open it, something flickered in the corner of my eye. I turned and saw a hooded figure leaning against a tree, about a quarter mile up the road. I squinted to try and make out whatever it was, but it had vanished.

"Boo!"

I jumped and let out a squeak before Ax rushed up beside me and pulled me into him by my waist. I giggled and placed one of my hands on his chest, the other brushing his brown hair out of his face.

"You scared me!"

"I'm as loud as an ox, how did you not hear me?" His gray eyes twinkled.

I gestured up the road. "I was focused! I thought I saw something up there—" but Ax very rudely interrupted me by dipping me and kissing me with a loud smack.

I laughed as he stood me upright.

"What do you think?" He grinned, looking at the house.

"It's perfect. Absolutely perfect." I said, throwing my arms around him. "I can't believe this is real! Pinch me, I must be dreaming."

He pinched me in a place that made me blush and giggle again. "By the way, Callie and Del should be over shortly. She's bringing us dinner tonight."

"Perfect." Ax raised an eyebrow at me, his gaze becoming more intense. "What do you say to *breaking in* the new house after everyone leaves?"

I opened my mouth in mock shock. "Good sir, don't be indecent!"

"Fine—I'll let *you* be then."

A car pulled up and I could see my sister through the windshield. She smiled at me and pointed to the phone she was holding to her ear. The back door of the car opened and closed, and a flash of dark coppery hair came racing towards us.

"Uncle Aaaaaxxxx!"

Ax scooped the girl up and threw her into the air, her squeals of delight making us all grin.

"Hey kiddo!"

"We brought dinner and dessert!" Del giggled, grinning so wide we could see all her missing teeth. "Pasta and Nutella rolls! Hi Auntie!"

"Nutella rolls?" I said, catching my niece's hand. "My favorite."

"Mine too."

"You and your Nutella." Ax gave Del a noogie and she laughed before she threw her arms around Ax's shoulders but smiled at me as he turned away. "Can we see your house?"

"You want to see our house?" Ax asked her. "It's a maze of boxes. Are you brave enough to find your way to the kitchen?"

Del nodded and started giggling again as Ax put her down and raced her to the house.

I smiled after them.

Truly, everything was perfect. Utterly sublime.

Oh, right. Mailbox.

I opened it and my stomach erupted in butterflies when I spotted an envelope in it. There was no address on it, but my name was in bold letters on the front.

I opened it.

Glad you're back.

Nothing else.

I turned the letter over, but it was blank on the other side too.

That's weird.

"Hey, Delphina? I need you!" Ax called from the house.

"Coming!" I jogged to the house but stopped at the door and looked at my sister. She was still on the phone and waved at me to go inside without her. I nodded but something flickered again at the corner of my eye. I looked up the road again before entering the house.

The figure was back, leaning against the tree. A chill went down my spine. In my bones I felt sure of something.

That whoever that was, was watching.

Watching the house.

Watching me.

18 WILLOW

I HAD Paxton bring us back to the police station as soon as we left the ME's office. After scanning the case file Solomon printed out for us and doing a quick Google search, I had a theory. After giving Chief Alvarado a quick run-down of our time at the ME's office, we asked him to bring Tony into the interrogation room again.

Tony had been leaning against the table when the door opened, but he sat back as I entered the room, Paxton behind me with a file under his arm. He followed us with his eyes as we sat down at the table.

Tony sat as far back from the table as he could and slouched in his chair so that his graying hair hung in curtains around his face.

"They see what they wanna see."

His voice caught me by surprise. "What was that?"

"People see what they want to see," he said again. "You asked me last time why I was content with letting people view me as a monster. 'Cause there's no point in trying otherwise. People will see and believe what they want, no matter how much you try to change their minds. It's a waste of time and I don't care to waste mine. Speaking of wasting time, let's get this over with."

I raised my eyebrows.

"It's not like you're going anywhere," Paxton said. "You're lucky Deputy Lox isn't pressing charges."

Tony huffed.

"But that's not why we're here," I said.

"No, you're here on account of that poor little lady who was butchered to death." Tony turned those sharp eyes to me again, showing me the rage building behind them. "Everyone knows I was part of that group of blood-obsessed fiends so it only makes sense that I must have had something to do with that girl's death. You think I'm crazy and that I might as well confess to everything I know about it now?"

Interesting. He used singular verbiage. Not proof, but indicative that he didn't know anything about the second body.

I sat forward, putting my arms on the table. "Not at all."

Tony snorted. "Sure."

"I'm being quite sincere, Mr. Vermont."

Tony froze. "What... what did you call me?"

"We looked through the records and files of a case from about fifteen years ago. We think you're Antonio Vermont. Or should I say *Dr.* Antonio Vermont? Graduated from Washington State Medical School in 1995, been practicing in Seattle ever since, until you disappeared over fifteen years ago. You turn up fifty miles away from Seattle in the compound of some deranged individuals, and yet once free, you don't return to Seattle. No family, few friends, and no one comes looking for you. You choose to stay living out in the woods in this podunk town, not even allowing your 'missing person' status to be updated."

Tony had looked down at the mention of no one looking for him.

"All those years ago, the bodies of the victims were examined. And what was recorded was that some of the bodies looked like they had had their limbs literally hacked off. Then there were those who were missing limbs, but the wounds looked as if it were done by a professional. A surgeon, even."

Tony's jaw tightened.

"You know what I think?" I leaned forward. "I think you were given the choice—to help the cult or become a victim yourself."

I paused but Tony just sat there, rigid and avoiding eye contact, so I continued.

"Most people can't imagine what it must be like to be put in that kind of position. Most people can't understand what it's like to have to fight for your life like that. But I do."

Paxton reached under the table and touched the side of my leg very briefly. The room was still and cool but to me, it was beginning to feel a little stuffy. I started to feel hot.

"It's hell... unlike anyone can imagine. And there's no escape. So when you find something that ensures your survival, you grab hold of it and don't let it go, no matter how twisted it is or how guilty it makes you, or how much of your soul you sacrifice for the chance to see the sun another day."

Tony, avoided my gaze, but tilted his head. As if he was hearing what I was really saying. His chest started to rise and fall a tiny bit faster.

"We're not here to grill you about the past, Tony. We're just trying to find out what happened to these young women. That's all."

Tony looked up then. "There's more than one?"

Paxton opened the file and slid pictures from both crime scenes in front of Tony. "Can you tell us anything?"

Tony looked at the pictures for a long time.

After a while, his eyes started to fill with tears.

"It's been a long time since anyone's called me Dr. Vermont," he said, his voice thick with phlegm. "I didn't want to. They made me... and they *needed* a doctor. Too many of *them* were dying."

I glanced over and saw Paxton's hand flying across his notepad.

"They called themselves the Limbless Ones. They killed everyone. But I... I *survived*." He looked up from the pictures. "Apart from them, I was the only survivor, correct?"

"That's what we read in the case notes," I said.

He paused. His face twitched.

"That's... incorrect. There was one more who escaped."

I felt my heart rate skyrocket. I looked at Paxton and saw my excitement and trepidation mirrored.

"Can you tell us—"

"I..." His eyes darkened as sadness and possibly shame crossed his face. "No. I...I don't remember. Please, don't ask me any more questions." Tony put his head in his hands.

"But—"

I put my hand on Paxton's shoulder, giving him a look.

"Very well. Thank you for your time, Dr. Vermont." I stood. "We'll talk more soon."

I left the room, holding the door open for Paxton. He followed behind me.

"Why did—"

"You can't force a confidence from anyone, especially from someone as traumatized as that man," I said. My hands felt gummy after I had wiped the sweat from them. "We'll ask him more questions later. I need some air right now."

We walked back up the hall together, into the lobby. The automatic doors opened and as I stepped into the parking lot, my body relaxed. Everything had started to feel claustrophobic inside.

We walked a little ways down the sidewalk so we weren't standing in the way of the lobby doors. I enjoyed the light misting of rain. Paxton started pacing beside me.

"He knows something."

I crossed my arms, looking at the ground as I replayed our conversation with Tony in my mind's eye. "I agree. But pushing him then could have possibly been detrimental. We'll need to go back and question him again, and soon. In the meantime, I think that we'll need to—" I stopped when I caught the look on Paxton's face.

I turned to see that he was looking at.

Leaning against a small Ford Fusion across the parking lot was the young woman from the coffee shop this morning. When she saw us, she stood and walked over.

She cast a glance my way before giving her whole attention to Paxton.

"I'm sorry to interrupt your day," she said.

Her hair was pulled back now and I could see her intelligent face and keen eyes. Her voice was sweet, and it quavered as she spoke. "Are... are you Paxton Holt?"

I looked at Paxton and saw him tighten his jaw. He took a deep breath and let it out before saying "I am."

The girl's lips pressed together, and her eyes started shining.

Paxton bit his lip, his own eyes glassing over.

The two of them held each other's gaze for a moment longer before they came together, her head in the crook of his neck and his hand over the back of her head. Almost like a father and daughter embracing.

I didn't want to spoil the moment but after a few seconds, I cleared my throat. What the hell was going on?

The two of them broke apart. The girl quickly wiped her eyes and Paxton gave me a look that was filled with such a mix of joy and regret that it was painful to observe.

"Willow, I would like you to meet my niece, Delphi."

19 HOLT

"You TOLD me you don't have any siblings."

"You're right. But my wife did." I turned from Willow, noticing her eyes having widened slightly at my admission, back to my niece.

My niece whom I hadn't seen or talked to in ten years.

She was in a thick coat, her ponytail catching in the fur lining. Her cheeks were pink but her fingers were white and bloodless from the cold.

She looked *just* like her.

I had thought that before, when I'd seen her in Cobain's. But seeing her up close was even more disarming.

She had always looked like her aunt, but the resemblance now was uncanny. Only her eyes were different—hazel, rather than cobalt blue. At the moment, her brow was scrunched up from confusion, anger, or disbelief. Perhaps all three.

"It's been so long." She stepped back another step and looked up at me, her eyes now red, her mascara starting to run along the edges.

"How did you know we were here?" I asked her.

"After I saw you in Cobain's, I wasn't sure if it was really you or not. But I heard you talking and I saw the badge on your side." Her voice caught. "FBI, just like you always wanted. I figured you were staying at The Glades so I called them to confirm it was you. And then I called the PD to ask where you were."

"Ever the little detective." My grin felt watery.

A half-smile formed on her lips before her face screwed up again. "Why did you leave? How could you leave without saying goodbye to me? How come you never answered any of my letters or messages? I mean, what the hell, Uncle Ax?" Her tone got progressively angrier as she spoke, until she stood a few feet back from me, her fists balled and her eyes flashing.

"Del—"

"No, I want answers dammit. I didn't just lose her, I lost you too and I want to know why. I know that's not a fair equation, I mean, you lost your *wife*, but... I had to lose both my aunt and uncle in one fell swoop." She sniffled for a moment, her eyes softening but brimming with tears. "But now you're here and I need to know if you're back or... or not." She took a deep breath.

It felt as if a weight had been put onto my neck and I hunched under the intensity of her gaze. Regret filled me to the point my fingers tingled with the rush of it.

"Delphi, I..." I bit my lip. I had one chance with this. I could not mess it up. "I don't know what to say. There's nothing I *can* say. I have no excuse, other than it was too painful. Losing her... losing her was the worst thing I've ever experienced. Being here in Marlborough hurt too much. Everything, every street corner, every brick reminded me of her and I couldn't stand it anymore. When the investigation went cold and I knew nothing more could be done, I left. I couldn't face saying goodbye to you because it felt too final. Like, if I said goodbye, I knew I'd be saying goodbye to her too. I couldn't face that." I shook my head.

"I have no excuse for not reaching out to you after the fact, though. I know how hollow it sounds, but I am sorry."

Del looked at me, her eyes narrowed. "I want to believe you. I've really missed you. Mom has too. We needed you when dad—" Her voice caught and another tear ran down her cheek but she wiped it away. "So all I want to know is... are you back or not?"

I clenched my jaw. I had never wanted to come back to Marlborough again. But to have a relationship with my niece? That, I did want. Cowardice had not only prevented me from confiding everything in Willow, but also prevented me from reaching out to the only family I had left.

But I didn't know how to tell her that without it sounding wrong.

"At least until the investigation is over?" Del said, jumping on my hesitation.

I nodded quickly. "At least until the investigation is over."

Del's shoulders relaxed. She looked over at Willow, a sheepish smile growing on her face. "This is all very dramatic. Sorry about that."

Willow blinked, as if coming out of a trance. "Oh, no. I mean, yes. I mean, um, it's okay."

"Hi, I'm Delphi Augur." Del stepped forward, reaching out her hand to Willow.

"I'm Willow. Um, Dr. Willow Grace, but you can just call me Willow."

"Wait, you're the cult expert lady?" Delphi blushed. "I'm sorry, I didn't mean for that to sound so callously blasé."

Willow let the kindest smile form on her lips, one I was grateful to see at a moment like this. "No, you're right. I am the cult expert lady."

"One of my friends took your class at Conifer College. Her name's Caroline?"

"Oh, yes!" Willow's shoulders eased. "She was one of my best students. You're not supposed to have favorites but... she was one of mine."

"That's great!"

An awkward pause ensued. Both women turned to me.

"Would you consent to coming to coffee with me and my mom tonight?" Del asked so fast it sounded like one word. "She gets off in a little bit. She'll want to see you. I don't wanna push I just—"

"Yes," I said. I simultaneously did and didn't want to go, but I glanced at Willow. She didn't know the whole story yet, but I knew that as soon as she did, she would insist I go. "This is an active case we're working on but everyone needs a coffee break."

Del's face lit up and her resemblance to Delphina deepened even further, as did the aching in my heart. "You look just like her," I said quietly.

She hung her head slightly and said, "Mom says that all the time." Just then her phone dinged, and she looked down as she pulled it out of her pocket. I watched her tap in the passcode, before realizing I had been staring and looked away. She frowned at her phone and started backing away to her car. "I have to go. Tonight at Cobain's?"

"I'll be there."

She gave me a leery look.

"I promise. This is *not* goodbye."

The corners of her mouth lifted again, before a glazed look came over her face.

"You're going to find the one, you know."

"What?"

"The one who's responsible."

I frowned. "What do you mean?"

The glazed looked on her face lifted. A swift grin flitted over her face before she spun towards her car, putting her phone to her ear as she did.

Puzzled, I watched as she got into the car, pulled out, and drove away.

Then I felt the weight of two eyes on the back of my head.

"That last bit was weird but... she's lovely."

I closed my eyes and took a deep breath. When I opened them, I turned to Willow, holding out my hands. "Willow, I—"

I stopped in my tracks, tilting my head slightly in a silent question. She was holding her hands up, her eyes unfocused. I stood there, waiting for her to say something.

"Paxton," she said after a minute. "I don't want to push you. I mean, we *just* talked about that but—" She bit her lip, preventing herself from speaking.

I could see the cogs turning in her head. All the anxiety, fear, and confusion over the last few days were about to overflow into whatever she was going to say and I could tell it was taking a tremendous amount of self-control for her to not lash out. She took a long, deep breath.

"But could you *please* explain what in the absolute hell is going on?"

20 WILLOW

His niece.

His wife's sister's kid.

His wife's sister.

His *wife*.

Yet, my head wasn't spinning. I didn't feel like my whole world was about to collapse. I didn't think I had misheard or that I was going crazy.

To be honest, I kind of felt validated, but in a numb sort of way.

Things... things were finally starting to make some sense. All of it, from him not wanting to come back to Marlborough, to him being distant, to him seemingly not wanting to take things further between us.

It all had to do with his wife.

What had happened to her? Delphi had said that she had lost an aunt and an uncle in one fell swoop. Had they been happy?

All these thoughts tumbled around like shoes in a dryer in my mind, each new thought like the shoe hitting the drum. My head ached.

"Willow, I... I owe you an explanation."

No kidding is what I wanted to say, but I raised my eyebrows in expectation instead.

Paxton raised one of his hands slightly, as if preparing to ward off a blow. "Let me grab something from the car, and I will explain everything."

I realized I was balling my fists. I unclenched them, wiping the sweat on my sides, and took another deep breath. I nodded and followed him to the car.

He jogged ahead of me, using his key to open the trunk from afar. By the time I caught up to him, he was pulling out that small briefcase I had noticed that was tucked in the back. I realized it had always been there and I always looked at it when I grabbed things from the trunk, but I had never put much thought into it. He picked it up, closed the trunk, and marched towards a little covered seating area along the side of the police station. It had several benches and a few picnic tables underneath.

He put the case down on one of the tables but didn't sit. He started pacing, rubbing a hand across his face.

I checked to make sure it wasn't wet before sitting on the closest bench, wincing slightly at how cold the metal felt through my pants.

As I watched him pace, the questions in my mind starting boiling over again.

Why had he never told me? How recent had it happened? Was he worried to open up about a previous romantic relationship? I had been married previously, so it's not like I would have judged him for that, although his marriage had probably been a lot different than mine.

My ex-husband's face flashed across my mind. Demented with that evil smile he loved to wear, getting closer to me to caress my cheek or touch my hair. A shiver ran down my spine and I shook my head to be rid of the image. He was dead now. He couldn't hurt me anymore.

Or was that the issue? Had his ex-wife been abusive? Had they been married long? Had she been sick? Had... had he been the problem and she left him?

Was she dead?

Paxton stopped and ran a hand through his hair and grabbed a fistful at the back. He looked at me, narrowing his eyes. I could tell he was trying to figure out how to begin.

I gripped the bench on either side of my legs, leaning my weight into my outstretched arms.

I waited.

We were still like that for a while. It was quiet apart from the light sprinkling of rain on the pavement. I watched him, seeing the battle in his mind play out in the expressions crossing his face. He would look up at me, take a breath as though about to start, before looking away again. There was still so much he wasn't telling me.

I hated seeing him like this.

I took another deep breath.

This whole thing was so confusing. I hated that he, for whatever reason, couldn't or wouldn't confide in me. We had worked closely enough together for us to trust one another with our lives. I trusted him more than I trusted anyone. He brought me on as a consultant for the FBI, *to be his partner*, so I knew that he trusted me too. Trust, therefore, couldn't be the issue.

I looked at the pain written on his face and realized perhaps that was it: it was painful for him to talk about, even with me. And I understood that. If there was anyone who could understand not wanting to open up about their past, it was me.

So ultimately, I decided I wasn't angry. Maybe things would have been easier if he had shared, and maybe they wouldn't have. I would not be angry at him for choosing not to confide in me, especially seeing him like this. But, we had come to this picnic area to talk about it, and I was tired of waiting for him to begin. "So... she's why you hate being back in Marlborough so much."

Paxton nodded.

I turned to face him. "How come you didn't say something? We didn't have to take this case. I would have understood, you know that more than anyone."

"She's dead." Paxton's voice was flat and dry as paper. "Just seemed silly to avoid a case and its jurisdiction because the memories associated are painful. I've been able to compartmentalize since it happened, so I should be able to now."

I bit my lip. After another moment of silence I asked, "How long?"

"Nearly ten years."

"That's... that's rough."

"Don't pity me, Willow."

"Hey." My tone made Paxton look back at me. "Paxton, all this time, all I've wanted is to be there for you, but I didn't know how to be because you kept and keep shutting me out. Things have been off between us ever since coming here and I didn't know why until now. I do, in fact, understand what this kind of pain feels like. As I've already said, you know that better than anyone."

The annoyance that had flared morphed into shame on Paxton's face. He looked at the ground.

I stood up and walked right up to Paxton so that I was looking up into his face.

"I just don't understand why you don't want to confide in me. Were you afraid I was going to judge you?"

Paxton ran his tongue over his teeth before sighing.

"I didn't tell you because... my wife is dead because of me. And it's all my fault." His voice caught on the last word and his eyes glassed over.

I felt my own eyes well up at the sight of him so close to tears. "Paxton, there has to be more to it than that. I know you. You would never let anything happen to anybody, much less your own wif—"

"You're wrong." Paxton paced away to the corner of the covered area, lightly hitting the side of the pole with his fist. "My wife's not just dead, Willow." He shook his head. I could see him clench his jaw before he said, "She was murdered."

My stomach dropped to my feet, and the writhing worms I felt in the showroom came back. I slowly sat back down on the bench.

"What... what happened?"

Paxton took a deep breath. "We met in college and hit it off right away. Cliché as it is, she took my breath away." Paxton leaned against the pole and turned back to me. "Didn't take long for us to get hitched. Just thought, why the hell not? Why wait?" He shoved his hands in his pockets. "Anyways, after we graduated, she wanted us to live here in Marlborough while I was in training for the FBI. The commute from here to Seattle was annoying, but it was only until I was done, and it didn't take very long. But after we moved to Marlborough, things got... strange. She kept feeling like something was off, like... someone was watching her."

His face screwed up then. He swallowed hard before continuing.

"It's not that I didn't *believe* her. I brushed her off, convinced her she was just stressed from the move, getting married, getting settled into our new lives. Starting her new job and so on. That's enough to fray anyone's nerves. I made sure our home was secure, but I didn't think much else of it.

"Then, one night, I came home from classes. I had gotten out early and wanted to surprise her since the last few nights I'd gotten home late. So I didn't call ahead to let her know I was coming home, like I usually would have. We were going to have hot chocolate that night, so I stopped to pick up the ingredients. I got home and about leapt from the car to go inside, expecting her to be startled, then jumping up and running to me... but I got to the front door and it was open." He paused and clenched his jaw.

"I called out to her, expecting her to respond. Maybe she was in the bathroom or had just stepped outside for a minute. I had my conceal-carry license so, just in case, I pulled out my revolver, and I slowly went inside. When I got to the kitchen..." his voice caught and he paused again. "There was so much blood. She was lying on the floor in our kitchen. It looked like she had fallen onto the knife she had been using to make dinner, but what are the odds of that happening? I just stood there, looking at her. It was like my mind had completely disconnected from my body and I couldn't process what I was looking at for what felt like an eternity. When I could move again, obviously I called 911. But it was too late. She'd lost too much blood and was losing more on the spot. I must have gotten there not too long after it happened. There might have been a chance if I hadn't just stood there. Maybe I would have gotten there in time if I'd have called her first, like I normally did."

"None of that was your fault." I said, as gently as I could.

He continued as if he hadn't heard me. "Later, the autopsy found bruises on her chest, hip, and arm, as if she had been pushed and tried to catch herself. Nothing else was found, no evidence of a struggle otherwise. No fingerprints of the perpetrator. Nothing."

Paxton looked at the briefcase on the table next us. He opened it and I was surprised to see it contained a single file, overflowing with documents. After confirming the picnic table was dry, he placed the file down and opened it.

He picked up the top picture. I watched his face closely as he looked at it and saw that wall come up again. As if he was re-encasing all his emotions.

"This is her." He handed me the picture. "Her name's Delphina."

I took it. There were two people, a young man holding a young woman damsel-in-distress style. Both of them were wearing deep blue graduation robes. At first, I thought the young woman was Delphi, but after a few seconds, I saw some differences. Delphi and this woman were both stunning, with the same dark coppery hair, the same button nose and elegant chin with a few instances of adult acne. But the woman in the picture had cobalt eyes and bigger lips. She held her diploma in one hand above her head. Her other arm was around the young man's shoulders.

The young man was a younger Paxton. His hair was still the same brown, but it was much longer in this picture. A few strands were hanging in his face. He was grinning wider than I had ever seen him smile. He was holding his diploma between the fingers of the same hand that was cupped under the woman's knees.

I looked down at the file and saw the picture underneath. My throat tightened at the grotesque image.

The same young woman lay on her back in the kitchen, a pool of blood formed beneath her. Her eyes were wide open. I could see the handle of a knife cut off by the edge of the picture.

I looked back at the graduation picture and my eyes brimmed with tears. They looked so happy.

All for it to end with her dead on their kitchen floor. The trauma this man had kept under the surface all this time must have been indescribable.

"It's all in there," Paxton said. "Feel free to look through it. I don't want to hide anything from you anymore."

I looked up and saw him looking away. He was leaning over with both hands outstretched against the table to support his weight.

I put the pictures down and put my hands on his shoulders.

He looked at me. His nose was flaring as he took in deep breaths. I could see his chest rising and falling. "I should have told you. I guess I was just... I don't know. I don't want to talk about her because I failed her. I failed to keep her safe. I failed to solve her case. I just didn't want to see the way you looked at me when you found out and I'm—" He stopped when I put my hand on his cool cheek.

"You thought I would think any differently about you because of this? You lost your *wife*. A wife you deeply loved." He shut his eyes tight and grabbed my hand on his face with his own. "I wish you had told me, but think differently of you? No. But I am so sorry that you had to go through that."

Paxton clenched his jaw again. Then he pulled me into an embrace, his face buried in the crook of my neck. I felt his body shake. The side of my neck began to dampen with his tears.

I put one arm around his shoulders and the other at the base of his neck, rubbing my fingers through the shorter hair there.

"I'm here," I whispered, "And I'm not going anywhere."

We stood there, holding each other for a few minutes before he pulled back but didn't let go of me. "I'm sorry. I'm sorry I didn't tell you. I'm sorry that I'm a mess. I've been broken since she died so I'm sorry that this is the version of me that you get."

I looked up at him. "I'm broken too. Maybe... maybe our broken pieces can fit together, and we can create something new. *This*"—I poked his chest lightly with my index finger—"is the version of you that I've... fallen in love with."

His eyes bore into mine. "You've fallen in love with me?"

"Why do you think I want to have sleepovers with you?"

"Can't imagine. Boys stink and girls have cooties, don't you know?"

I laughed and he grinned, still holding me at the waist. He looked at my mouth, hesitating for only a second before pressing his lips to mine.

Both of us melted into it. Did it heal our brokenness? Did it magically make everything better?

No.

But I felt like, maybe, he and I were finally on the same page.

21 WILLOW

"Holt? Grace?"

We broke apart at the sound of our names being called. I felt my face warm as Chief Alvarado walked towards us. His eyebrows were raised, and he had a slight twinkle in his eyes.

"Have you two been out here smooching the whole time?"

Paxton cleared his throat and I wanted to crawl into a hole.

Alvarado chuckled "Wanted an update on what Tony said."

"Ah, yes sir." Paxton placed the file back into the briefcase. "I'll go put this in the car and be right in. Go on without me."

He walked back to the car with the briefcase, his ears red.

My face felt even warmer as the chief and I walked inside, but I couldn't help but laugh when he leaned over to me and whispered, "I wondered if the two of you were an item."

"We try to keep it on the down-low. Won't happen again."

"Cases are stressful. It's good to have an... outlet." He grinned at me and waggled his eyebrows.

My face reddened as he gestured for me to proceed through the automatic doors to the lobby.

He led me past the receptionist desk to the small, orderly offices behind. I realized that I had not yet been in the main offices of the Marlborough PD, so

I took the time to observe the new surroundings. Multiple desks were set up in the center of the room. Along one wall was a large TV screen. An empty holding cell in a far corner. A glass-walled office, similar to McCannon's, was to the left and I suspected it to be Alvarado's.

The small police force were all working. A female deputy I had seen but not met was typing away at a computer. Another more androgynous-looking deputy was pouring over some paperwork. I spotted Deputy Lox by the coffee station. He raised his mug to me when he saw me.

Paxton jogged in. His face was a tad flushed and he was a little out of breath. "Sorry about that."

"I was just about to tell Grace we have a small update about the puzzles," Alvarado said. He gestured to the deputy typing on the computer. "This is Deputy Atta Larson."

She smiled and nodded to us. Her hair was in a bunch of tiny braids, but the lot of them were in a neat bun on the back of her head.

"Larson, show us what you discovered."

She nodded again and pulled up a few images on her computer. "We scanned the puzzle pieces found at both crime scenes." She pointed to a scanner by her monitor.

I walked over to the scanner and asked, "May I?"

She nodded and I opened the top.

Two sections of puzzle were laid out on the counter in the picture. Both had sections of bright red with blue underneath. A part of one section was brown, but there wasn't enough of the puzzle to be able to tell what it was.

"We found a couple of potential matches," Larson said, pulling up a few images from a puzzle site. One was a picture of a red-striped building with a brown roof. The sky was a bright blue and flowery weeds surrounded the base of the building. She pulled up six more images, all with similar red stripes over a bright blue surface.

Paxton rubbed the back of his neck. "But we don't know which one?"

The chief shook his head. "I did say it was a small breakthrough."

I rubbed my lips with the back of a finger. "I guess it's good to know the puzzle might not be one of a kind."

Someone snorted and I turned to see Lox had walked up behind us. He rolled his eyes at me and took a sip from his mug. "Basically, useless information."

Larson shot an annoyed look at Lox but said, "He's not wrong. Puzzle's a bit of a moot point. It might be able to tell us more if we had more of the pieces but..."

"We really don't want more pieces," I said.

"Exactly."

"Which prompts me to my next question," The chief said. "How'd things go with Tony?"

Everyone turned to face me and Paxton.

"We had a mini breakthrough too," Paxton said.

I nodded. "Tony said he wasn't the only one who'd escaped the cult all those years ago."

There was a pause.

"Do you know who?" Lox asked, taking another sip from his mug.

Paxton took a deep breath.

"We showed him the pictures from the crime scenes," I said, "And once he saw them... it was like he recognized what he was looking at. With no prompting he brought up there was another survivor but when we asked him who it was, he said he couldn't remember. Then he completely shut down on us."

"Maybe he *couldn't* remember?" Lox said.

Larson punched his side. "Would you stop playing devil's advocate for three seconds?"

Lox lost his balance as he side-stepped and spilled the remnants of his coffee all down my front.

Lox swore. "My bad, I didn't mean—"

"No, no, don't worry about it." I said, blinking rapidly and tasting sugary burnt coffee on my lips.

Larson handed me a fistful of napkins she pulled out of her desk drawer. "That's my fault, I'm sorry Dr. Grace."

I patted my front down, but I would need to change clothes. "It's no big deal. Anyways back to Tony, no, I don't think that's it. It's like... like he couldn't bring himself to tell us."

Lox rolled his eyes. "Respectfully and unfortunately, that doesn't do us any good, so we're back to square one."

"Or piece one, as it were," the chief said.

Paxton looked at his watch. "I have to drop off Willow and get to an appointment. We'll check in later."

The chief nodded to us as Paxton and I made our exit through the office, lobby, and front double doors.

"Again, sorry about your clothes!" Lox called behind us.

I waved as we walked through the automatic doors. A chill flashed over my body as the wind blew against my wet clothes.

"I can check in with McCannon while you're with Del and Callie tonight," I said as we got into the car.

"You think it will be okay?"

I looked up from buckling my seatbelt and saw Paxton biting his lip.

"It sounds to me like you'd like to reconnect with your family. And maybe it's the psychologist in me, but I think that it will be good for you. Maybe it will help you heal."

Paxton nodded.

I leaned across the center console. "I think it will be okay. And if it's not, you can at least say you tried."

Paxton nodded. Then he looked up at me and smiled. "Thank you."

"For what?"

"For not leaving me. Or making me feel small."

"Never."

He leaned across the center console too and kissed me. Then he put the car in drive and we pulled out of the parking lot.

I didn't just want to update McCannon.

I also wanted to read his wife's case file.

22 THE KILLER

They were all right there.

He was sitting in his car outside Cobain's. The coffee shop was a cage of memories.

He'd been sure to get here in time to watch the three of them reunite. He got a masochistic sense of satisfaction watching. It was like picking at a scab—it was satisfying to do, but it made the scarring worse. Watching what should have been his sparked a flame inside him.

Del had arrived first. She had come ten minutes early—something he knew she was prone to do—and she was now watching the road from her car, fiddling with her dark hair, and occasionally glancing in the mirror.

About five minutes later, Holt pulled in. He looked around the parking lot to find his niece. When he saw her, relief and apprehension flashed across his face.

Holt. He cursed the man's name. He remembered his shock when he had run into him in that very shop. What was *he* doing back here, after all these years?

Holt got out of his car and so did Del. The two of them came together in a quick embrace.

Even if his windows had been rolled down, he was too far away to hear their conversation.

But he watched their expressions. They were both nervous but cautiously happy to be there judging by them shifting their weight from foot to foot and sneaking glances at each other as if they were both afraid the other would vanish. Seeing them together again was like feeling the wound re-scab over.

A few minutes later, a van with darkened windows pulled in. Del had stiffened at the sight of the vehicle. She motioned to it and Holt looked at it, his brows furrowing and his stance becoming ridged.

Calliope Augur slid out of her vehicle, facing away from him so he couldn't read her expression. Her back was poker-stick straight as she walked up to Holt and Del.

The three of them stood there for about ten seconds, their mouths unmoving. Del's eyes jumped between her mother and Holt, biting her plump bottom lip.

Those lips. He felt a tingling all down his body.

Then Calliope stepped forward and embraced Holt, putting her arms around his shoulders. Holt looked somewhat surprised at the contact, but he melted into the embrace. He blinked rapidly, as though to get something out of his eye.

Del's eyes were shining. Her mouth was half upturned as if she was trying not to smile too hard.

A tingle slithered down his body. To see some semblance of that beloved smile again... It was enough to give him peace about the road ahead of him. The road was hard, harder than anything he had ever done.

Well... excepting that day.

Then Del dashed forward and flung her arms around the other two so that they were all in an insipid embrace, right in the middle of Cobain's parking lot.

Hatred and longing formed in his gut. *It should have been his.*

For a small eternity he watched the three of them, embracing and looking at one another and clearly trying not to cry. Then they broke apart and went inside Cobain's, each woman on either side of Holt. That bastard had no idea how lucky he was.

He continued waiting and watched the three of them approach the counter and order. Holt made a gesture towards the women, likely offering to cover the bill. As if he could win their trust back by buying a couple of measly coffees. The fool. Didn't Holt know that once trust was lost, it was gone for good? He did; and it still haunted him.

Soon, he would have the opportunity to mend what he had broken.

The three of them walked to the end counter. Del looked behind her and pointed to a table. Holt and Callie nodded. Del walked over to the table and sat at it. She unabashedly watched Holt and Callie as they waited for their drinks.

He could see Callie's face now. She looked wan and weary as she and Holt spoke. A few minutes later, the barista handed them their drinks, and Holt and Callie joined Del at the table. Callie sat next to her daughter and Holt sat across from them.

Del said something and the three of them laughed. The last vestiges of apprehension seemed to melt off everyone's faces.

That did it.

That flame turned into hellfire. A rage he hadn't felt in a long time seeped through him as he continued to watch, desperate to act.

They looked just the same as they always had. As if no time had passed. They were comfortable together. Happy, even.

For that, he loathed them. He loathed them for moving on with their lives as if *she* had never existed. As if *she* meant *nothing* to them.

Del looked just like her. She didn't know how lucky she was to have the face of an angel.

Only her eyes were different. She had hazel eyes.

Her mother though... Calliope had Delphina's eyes. The exact same cobalt blue ones.

She was lucky to have them. She didn't know how lucky.

And she never would.

Not until it was too late.

23 DELPHINA - TEN YEARS AGO

I WAS BEING WATCHED.

A prickle of intuition traveled down my neck and through my spine. This had been going on for months, ever since we had moved in. At first, I didn't think much of it, attributing it to nerves and tricks of the light or my own imagination.

Now, though? Now I wasn't so sure.

I didn't move from my spot at the stove, stirring my sauce. The smell of oregano and garlic, usually so enticing, did not spark the usual satisfaction this morning. My back faced the window on the wall opposite the stove. I thought I saw a shadow flash in my peripheral vision.

I slowed my stirring, straining my ears. All I could hear was the bubbling of the sauce and something... something else. What—

He grabbed my hips from behind.

I jumped and let out a small yelp. My body relaxed when he kissed my neck and the smell of his cologne calmed my nerves. I tapped the spoon against the pot to remove the excess before resting it on the pot's lip. I turned around to meet his lips with my own, wrapping my arms around him.

"Smells good." Ax said, smiling into my mouth before kissing me again. "Pasta sauce?"

I nodded. "Spaghetti's for dinner tonight. It's that recipe that has to simmer for six hours."

"I see that." He let me pull away so I could go back to tending the sauce. "Rare day off for you. You got anything going on today?"

"I got a new puzzle. I plan on working on that."

He rolled his eyes and smiled at me. "You and your puzzles."

I tilted my chin up at him. "This one is only five hundred pieces. Shouldn't take me very long."

Ax kissed the side of my head and walked over to the dining room table in the middle of the farm-style kitchen. I turned in time to see him point to another puzzle on the dining room table. "How about you finish this one first?"

"I'm bored of that one. I'll come back to it."

He rolled his eyes as he flopped some papers on top of the puzzle. He leaned over them. The morning light from the window behind him cast the papers in shadow.

"Whatcha looking at?" I asked, wiping my hands on my apron as I walked over.

"Just some case files for work. I was working on them after I got home last night."

I huffed.

He tore his eyes from the papers and saw my expression. His own softened as he stood and pulled me in by my waist. I allowed my head to rest on his shoulder as I wrapped my arms around him.

"I know, I know. I already work late nights and I'm sorry—"

"And I know you're sorry. But I also know what this training requires of you." I put my hand on his chest and felt his heart beating against my palm. "I just miss you. I always miss you."

He squeezed me tighter. "You're, like, the best wife."

Without letting go, I looked up at him and grinned. "I know." I brushed his dark hair off his forehead. I stepped back and brushed the wrinkles from his dress shirt before spotting a red blotch on his side.

"Oh shoot, I got sauce on your shirt!"

He looked down, his hair falling back onto his forehead. "Aww, this is my last clean shirt."

"It's not, there's another one on the ironing board." I said, pushing his hair out of his face.

He shot me a look, half annoyed half amused, before making his way to our bedroom, unbuttoning his shirt as he went.

I looked back down at the papers on the table, my shadow cast over them. I stood still, reading the files, when another shadow moved across the table. I whirled around, facing the big window head on. I looked out but saw nothing but our backyard. The grass was still trimmed from when Ax cut it this last weekend.

I leaned against the windowsill, watching the way the breeze made the high brown grass at the tree line sway, when I noticed where it looked like the high grass had been pushed to the side. Leading away from there and back towards the house were oval indentations in the grass on the lawn.

Were those footprints?

"You were right, there was one more on the board."

I jumped and turned to see Ax standing at the opposite end of the table, wearing a new shirt, his suit coat folded over his arm. He looked surprised to see me at the window.

"Whatcha looking at?" he asked me.

I looked over my shoulder out the window, about to point out the footprints when a deer walked through the yard, sniffing the grass. Indented footprints trailed behind it. "Nothing. I thought I saw something. Just a deer."

I had tried over the last few months to tell him of my concerns, but he had never seemed to take my worries seriously.

Ax nodded. "I gotta go, love."

"You always do." I walked over to him and helped him put his files back in order before carefully putting them in his briefcase.

"It's likely to be another late night, so don't wait up for me."

I groaned as I leaned my head back, but I smiled at him when he gave me that cute apologetic look he always did when he was trying to placate me. He scrunched his brows together and pulled his lips up in a comical frown.

"I'm sorry," he said as he picked up his stuff and I followed him to the front door. "I'll bring home some whipped cream and we can have hot chocolate by the fire when I get home. Deal?"

I wrapped one arm around his neck and ran the other through his hair again. "Dealio."

He gave me a big kiss. "Ugh, you are so beautiful. I love you. See you tonight!" He opened the door and I stood in the doorway as I watched him get into the car and drive away.

The breeze blew against my skin and goosebumps erupted on my arms. I looked up at the sky, unsurprised by the large expanse of uninterrupted gray coming in, the clouds quickly closing in the sun like a curtain being drawn. I could smell the rain in the air.

I closed the door behind me and locked it.

The prickle landed on the back of my neck again, and I went about the house and made sure all the windows were shut and locked too. I felt silly. The house was secure and nothing had ever happened. But I had a habit of taking precautions. Just in case. I was married to an FBI agent in training, after all.

Once that task was done, the tension left my shoulders.

I headed back to the kitchen and poured the sauce from its pot on the stove into a crockpot to slow cook until tonight. Then I made myself some hot tea. I glanced at the kitchen window and decided to draw the curtains. It wasn't likely someone would be watching me through the window, but it still helped settle my nerves once and for all.

I headed to the living room, situated to the left of the front door. The couches were arranged in an L with the TV along the back wall. There was a large dark coffee table in the center of the room. I placed my mug on a coaster, sat on the floor and pulled the puzzle from the bag I'd brought it home in yesterday. I opened it and got to work.

And that was how I spent my morning and afternoon, only stopping for an hour to make a no-rise bread and put it in the oven.

All was peaceful.

Until the doorbell rang.

It was so unexpected that I jumped, my hand jerking and knocking over a section of the puzzle. "Shit," I muttered, gathering the pieces into my palm and dumping them unceremoniously on the table. I got up and walked around the couch, heading to the front door. I looked through the peephole and was stunned by who I saw on the other side. I reached for the doorhandle, unlocked it, and threw it wide open.

"Rick?"

I hadn't seen him since my senior year of high school, at my going-away party before going to college.

I hadn't thought about him in ages. After the party, I had been too mad at him to try and reach out before I left. But once I had cooled down, I had regretted leaving in anger. I had tried to reach out to him, but he never responded. Classes started picking up and I didn't think about it again.

What on earth was he doing here?

"It's good to see you, Delphina." He had always been thin, but he looked especially gaunt now. His dark hair was greasy and hanging in his face. He looked up at me between the curtains of his hair and gave me that small smile I had grown fond of throughout our year working on puzzles together.

I had always felt bad for him. Poor kid was found on the side of the road, abandoned, cold and starving. He was put into foster care and ended up with the Smiths, some close family friends of ours. My mom had told me about him and encouraged me to be nice to him whenever I'd had the opportunity.

It wasn't hard. He had been like a drowning puppy. I'd never seen such a pitiful face. It was easy to pity him.

Until he had kissed me.

"What are you doing here?" I asked, wary.

He shrugged. "Ran into Callie not too long ago. She told me you had moved back into town."

"Oh, yeah." I rubbed the back of my neck, realizing I wasn't too pleased about my sister outing me like that. "I got a job working for the city. Just for the time being, you know?"

Rick nodded. Gosh, he was skin and bones, more so than when we'd been in high school. He looked like he could use a few square meals.

"How're your parents doing?" I asked. I hadn't had the chance to reach out to Laura and Jerry.

Rick lifted a shoulder. "Dunno. I moved out a while ago. Didn't keep in touch."

That explained why he was looking so peaky. Laura would never let a kid of hers go hungry.

"That's too bad." I didn't really know what else to say. It's not like we were friends anymore.

I noticed that he was holding a nice wooden frame.

I pointed at it. "What's that?"

He looked down at it as if he'd forgotten he was holding anything. "This uh... is a present for you. Can... can I come in?"

I hesitated. I didn't really want to let him in, but what would a few minutes hurt? "Sure, I guess." I turned around to lead him inside and talked over my shoulder. "I was just working a puzzle actually."

He stepped inside, looking around.

"Can I get you something to drink?" I asked.

He nodded and asked for water as we moved to the kitchen. I had been away from the pot long enough that I could smell the oregano again. It seemed to clear my mind. I busied myself getting a glass from the cabinet.

"Smells good," he said. I turned to see him still standing across the table, still holding the wooden frame.

"Just some spaghetti sauce. Here you go." I handed him the glass of water across the table. My oven beeped then, and I looked through its glass door.

Seeing a golden crust, I pulled the loaf out of the oven, placing it on the wooden cutting board by the stove. I turned to see him still standing across the table, still holding the wooden frame.

"So," I gestured at the box in his hands.

"It's for you."

I moved over to the other side of the table and looked at the frame more closely. Inside was a completed puzzle, one that I recognized.

"Oh my gosh. Is that the one I gave you before I left for college?"

I noticed he twitched at the mention of me leaving but his voice, so much lower than when we were kids, was steady. "Yeah, this is it."

"Wow. This was... really sweet of you. I'm surprised you kept it all these years."

"You shouldn't be... not really." He still held the frame. I noticed that the glass was loose, almost too small for the frame.

My tongue went dry and I wished I was holding something. Why did I suddenly feel nervous? It's just my old friend from high school. So why did the look in his eyes make my stomach twist?

"Delphina... listen."

Oh no.

"This wasn't a spur of the moment visit. I've been wanting to see you again for years. Ever since you left."

"Is that right?" I turned away and walked towards the bread on the cutting board. I didn't usually like to cut the bread when it was fresh out of the oven, but I felt better holding a knife. "I'm surprised to hear that. You had my number. You could have reached out."

He hesitated. "I can't deny that I was... I had a hard time forgiving you for leaving."

I frowned and glanced over at him. "I was going to college. It's not like that's unusual... or *wrong*." I put emphasis on the last word.

"No, but... you realize why I felt that way." He took a few steps closer to me. I wished he would put that frame down. I tightened my grip on my knife.

Oh *no*. I was starting to regret letting him in.

"It's 'cause... I... love you. I've always loved you."

The bread was burning me, but I didn't want to stop moving my hands. "That's... that's nice," was all I could manage as he took another step closer, behind me.

"I have *always* loved you." He was so close to me now I could feel his breath on my neck. "I've finally forgiven you and I'm ready for us to be together."

Shit.

I stayed put but cringed at feeling his body so close to mine. "I'm sorry Rick. I'm married. I haven't seen or heard from you in years. I don't feel that way about you at all. I thought the way I responded at my going away party was a clear indication of my romantic feelings for you." I maneuvered myself from between him and the counter and turned to face him.

He frowned at me. "You're... you're not taking me seriously at all, are you?"

"I am, I'm just being—"

"This is serious, Delphina."

"So is the fact that I'm married."

"Delphina—"

I crossed my arms against my chest, still holding the knife. "You, after years of no contact, come into *my* home that I have with *my husband* and have the audacity to accuse *me* of not being serious? You're crazy, right?"

"Don't call me crazy!" He pushed the wooden frame against my chest and the glass popped out of place. I jumped back, trying to grab the counter but slipped. The knife was still in my hand.

There was so much blood.

I pulled my hand away from the gash in my neck and saw it drenched in blood. *My* blood.

I gurgled and choked. "Ri—Rick...?"

He just stood there, mouth slack, still holding the frame in his hands, blood spattering against his shoes, pooling around the ground in front of him.

I slumped sideways, hitting my shoulder on something before I landed on the floor, my body at an angle facing up. I heard the clattering of pieces as I landed on the mess of blood beneath me. In my direct line of sight was the floor of the dining room and the white table and chair legs.

Wow. Dusty.

"Delphina!"

His face was blurry around the edges. "I'm sorry, I'm sorry, I'm sorry! Wait! I can fix this, I can—"

"Don't... touch... me..." I tried to say but I coughed and saw blood splatter on his face and the table leg beside him.

Oh. Oh, no.

I'm dying, aren't I?

Ax's smile flashed in my mind's eye. I'd never see him again.

"Delphina, wait, please I didn't mean it, I'm sorry—"

I looked up at him and I couldn't make out his face anymore. I couldn't remember it feeling so cold a moment ago.

"Damn... you."

His face was the last thing I ever saw.

24 WILLOW

THE EVENING WAS WEARING ON. After getting back to the motel room and updating McCannon on the case, I stripped off the dirty coffee-laden clothes and headed to the bathroom. I looked at myself in the mirror, at the dried coffee residue that was visible on my front.

It used to be hard to look in a mirror. I was afraid of what I would see. In my youth, I saw a scared girl, forced into a marriage I didn't want. As an adult, I saw a scared woman, terrified of being found. Now, I saw a woman who had been through a lot.

And come out stronger.

We would come out of this stronger, right?

I felt like everything was at a standstill. It seemed like we had exhausted every lead. All the witnesses had been questioned, all the clues followed up on, and we were no closer to finding out who killed these two girls. My brain felt like mush.

I turned on the shower, waited for the water to warm, and got in. I stood there with my eyes closed, feeling the hot water on my skin.

Chief Alvarado had called us on our drive to say he was overseeing the transport of Issie's remains back to her family. Dr. Solomon had been able to ascertain no further information from when we'd seen him. Paxton had then dropped me off and left for Cobain's to meet up with his niece and—Former? Ex? Old?—Sister-in-law.

I opened my eyes and looked around. The tub was yellowing. The minerals in the water had built up a layer of scum around the faucet, shower handle, and support handle. The shower curtain bar was bowed out, but the white curtain was limp and thin. I closed my eyes again and turned around, running my hands through my hair.

He had been married to the love of his life. Everything that he had told me, all the information I could find about her online with a quick Google search, had corroborated the picture forming in my head: Delphina Holt had been an amazing woman. Goosebumps rose on my arms and back despite the hot water

It's not that I was jealous. I really thought about that, but at the end of the day, it wasn't jealousy. It was envy. I envied Delphina.

Jealousy and envy aren't that different from each other, but jealousy often stemmed from resentment. I didn't resent her. How silly would it be to resent a woman I had never met? But I did envy her. I envied that she had been Paxton's first choice. That she had gotten to be with and enjoy that carefree Paxton, the one who had been goofy and unmarred by life. Unmarred by losing her.

I also felt regret. Regret that I hadn't met Paxton sooner. That we would never get to share those kinds of "firsts" together. That my own past had made loving me hard. That I was anxious, feared the worst, and was independent to my own detriment. That his past made it hard for him to open up. Regret that it was only from living through the lives we had that Paxton and I had met at all.

And yet, there was still a bond there. A strange kind of camaraderie between us that we could share only *because* of the lives and experiences that we had both endured. How strange and hard and weird and beautiful our experiences were.

I turned the shower off but stood still in the steam for a few minutes. I needed to look through her file. Perhaps it was masochistic, but I wanted to look at those pictures of her again. Is it strange that I wanted to feel the sting that he had loved someone before me but also honor her memory? But something else nagged at the back of my mind. Something that caused an alarm to go off in my head. But I couldn't quite put my finger on what.

I stepped out of the tub and wrapped one towel around my head and another around my torso. The bathroom was now so steamy that the mirror was clouded. I didn't bother to try and look in it again. I opened the bathroom door and walked into my room, shivering slightly from the change in temperature. There were two queen size beds, a nightstand in between them, an armchair, a desk with a TV on top and a chair pushed in. The carpet was a dark green.

Grabbing my robe from the tiny makeshift closet in the corner, I dropped my towels and slid my arms into the sleeves of the robe, noting its rough texture.

The briefcase lay closed on my desk. Paxton had put the briefcase in my legroom in the car rather than back in the trunk. A further invitation for me to come in. He hadn't batted an eye when I'd grabbed the briefcase and exited the car with it. He'd meant it when he'd said I could look through her file.

I sat on my bed, looking at the briefcase. I wanted to properly process all the information that I now had about Paxton. As much as I was happy —*relieved*—he had shared, his past was weighty. And he had had to carry that burden alone. Much like I had with my own past until I had met him. He had not flinched at the weight of my baggage. I would not flinch at the weight of his. I cared about him too much to balk at this. I thought about the kiss we had shared after I had told him I had fallen in love with this version of him.

The memory made me smile.

I brought the briefcase to my bed, carefully opening it and leafing through the pages until I found the stack of photos.

There were about a dozen photos. I had already seen the top two, but I looked at a few more.

The first few were of just Delphina. One was a high school graduation picture. She was grinning, wearing a teal robe and cap and holding her diploma tucked underneath her arm. Another was of her eating an ice-cream cone, her nose covered in chocolate and giving the camera a beady side-eye. The next was a college graduation picture, her pose similar to the high school graduation photo but I could tell she was just a few years older. I was struck by how much

Delphi looked like her aunt. They had the same face shape, same nose, same soft sweet smile. No wonder Paxton had done several double takes. Delphi now was likely the same age as her aunt in this picture, probably 22 or 23.

The next picture was of Delphina and Holt together at their wedding. They were sitting together, Paxton grinning at the camera while she was grinning at him. She wore a plain white dress with a cheap looking veil pinned under an up-do, and Paxton wore a suit that didn't fit him properly. Two broke kids who had just graduated college, but were madly in love. The happiness on both of their faces was obvious. The look she gave him in this photo was nothing less than pure adoration.

That stingy ache started forming in my heart again.

The next picture was of Paxton, another woman, and Delphina holding a little girl in front of a cute little brick house. My guess was that the girl was Delphi, and the woman was Callie, Delphi's mother. The house was probably the one Delphina and Paxton had moved into after college. Even here, the resemblance between Delphi and Delphina was striking.

I let the photos slide back to the top two.

"You don't know me," I said to the picture of Delphina and Paxton in their graduation robes. "But... Paxton's with me now. If you had lived... well, I hope he wouldn't be. I hope the two of you would have worked out. I wish you could see where he is now. He's an FBI agent. He's solved so many cases. He's even recruited me. How crazy is that? I'm just a college professor."

My eyes unfocused. "I'm more than a college professor. And he saw that. And... I think he cares for me. I think that I'm the first person he's truly cared about since you."

I looked back at the photo and ran the tip of my finger over Delphina's hair. "He's gonna be okay. I'm going to take care of him. He means... he means the world to me. So thank you. Without you, there wouldn't be us."

I felt a mixture of foolishness and relief. The picture couldn't hear me but I wanted to acknowledge her. She was a big part of Paxton's story and if I tried to ignore her, I would be ignoring a part of Paxton.

Sure, it hurt. It hurt to know there was another before me. But just because Paxton had loved someone else a long time ago, didn't mean what we have right now wasn't real.

I took a deep breath and released it slowly.

We were going be okay.

I looked down at the next picture, the picture of Delphina's corpse. I tried to imagine what it must have been like for Paxton to come home and find her on the floor in a pool of blood. I thought about the victims and felt my stomach start to writhe with worms again. It had been horrible seeing those girls. It must have been hell finding her.

I leafed through the file and found other pictures of the scene. From what I could tell, they'd had an open floor plan. The kitchen was a large open plan with the dining room table in the middle, opening out into the living room and front door. The picture showed a clear view of both the kitchen and living room. The couches were set up in an L shape around the TV, a coffee table in the center. An unfinished puzzle waited for its owner to come complete it.

I flipped through the rest of the pictures, closer-ups of each room in the house and something striking stood out to me.

Puzzles.

There were puzzles in every picture. A shelf in the living room was stacked with puzzle boxes. Even the dining room table had an incomplete puzzle on top of it. It was a picture of a forest, with only a few sections in the middle that had not yet been filled.

I flipped back to the picture of Delphina lying on her dining room floor. There were red puzzle pieces on the floor under the table and a few on her body.

That couldn't be right.

I looked at the other pictures. The puzzle pieces on the dining room table were all green and browns. Not a single section was red.

The puzzle on the coffee table was a picture of a dolphin mid flip over the ocean. No red in that puzzle either.

I looked back at the red puzzle pieces. Were they red because of blood? No.

Then I noticed a section of puzzle still intact in the far corner of the picture way under the dining room table. I turned the photo nearly upside down to see it properly.

This section of puzzle had red lines on top of bright blue with a solid stripe of brown in it.

Just like the puzzle sections found at the crime scenes.

25 WILLOW

A KNOCK on the door made me jump and a bunch of the pictures fell to the floor.

"Willow?" A muffled voice came through the door and I ran over and looked through the peep hole. "Hey, it's Paxton. I wanted—"

I flung the door open. Paxton's fist was still poised to knock and he looked startled as I grabbed his arm and pulled him inside.

"I have to show you something," I said as I dragged him to the bed.

"What—"

"I found something. In the pictures." I said as I started picking up the ones that had fallen to the carpet.

"Willow, I've looked at those pictures hundreds, maybe thousands of times. I was never able to find a lead."

"But I might have."

We looked at each other in intense silence before he responded with a curt nod and said, "Show me."

I stood up and laid the pictures out on the bed. "I noticed puzzles in each photo. Every room in the house either had puzzle boxes stacked, or an unfinished puzzle laying out."

Paxton gave me a nod like he was guiding me to get to the point. "Yes, Delphina loved puzzles. Was her favorite hobby."

I held up one of the pictures of the dining room scene, with the red and blue puzzle pieces in the corner. "There are puzzle pieces on the floor. They're all red. None of the puzzles she was currently working on, at least in the dining room or living room were red."

Paxton's brow furrowed. He turned and sat on my desk chair, folding his arms.

"They aren't bloodstained either." I pointed to a section of the photo, making sure to block her body from view with my hand. "Look at the corner of this picture. Do you see the cluster of puzzle pieces?"

Paxton squinted. He looked for a few seconds and his chest started to rise and fall a little faster.

"I can't believe I've never noticed that. She had so many puzzles, it never occurred to me that those were out of place. We had never found any conclusive evidence of someone being there. No footprints, fingerprints, anything. No one believed me when I insisted it was a murder and not a freak accident."

"But do you know what else?" I said. "Don't the colors of those pieces look familiar?"

His eyes widened, and his mouth fell open.

"There's no way of knowing for sure," I said. "But they look like a match for—"

"—the puzzles found at the other crime scenes." Paxton finished my sentence. He looked away, his eyes darting back and forth as if looking at something in his mind's eye. "There might be a way to check."

I sank onto the bed. "What do you mean?"

"I mean that those puzzle pieces, along with the knife, were brought into evidence. Here, in Marlborough." He looked back at me. "If they're still there—"

"We can see if they're connected."

We stared at each other for a long moment.

And I realized I was wearing nothing but a robe that was now gaping open at the front. Paxton seemed to realize at the same time because I saw his eyes look down before snapping back to my face.

I jerked the robe tightly closed and crossed my legs but that raised the bottom hem of the robe half-way up my thigh. "Oh." I felt myself blushing. "Sorry I—"

Paxton watched the movements. He raised his eyebrows at me, a small grin forming on his face.

I jumped up. "I'm sorry, I didn't-I can-I'm gonna just—"

He stood up and came over to me, putting his hands on my arms to stop me before I could scurry back to the bathroom. "Don't be embarrassed," he glanced down at the pictures on the bed. "As weird as it is to say this with my dead wife's murder scene pictures lying on your bed, it's okay. You look cute." He looked uncomfortable, but he attempted a smirk anyway.

"Thanks, I, uh, I'm going to go get dressed."

Paxton nodded, clearing his throat and pulled his phone out of his pocket. "I'll call ahead to see if they'll get the stuff out of evidence." He turned around and faced the hotel door as I grabbed my clothes from my open suit case in the corner and dashed to the bathroom. I dropped the robe and started getting dressed at top speed.

As I pulled my shirt over my head, I came back out of the bathroom and I caught the end of a sentence. "... from case #328, yes. We think that they might be connected with the current case."

I slid into my shoes. I grabbed my coat and came up beside him. Feeling my touch, he nodded at me, keeping the phone pressed to his ear.

I put the case file back into the briefcase and grabbed it.

"Perfect, we'll be right there." Paxton hung up. "Larson and Lox are still there. Told us to get to the station ASAP."

26 WILLOW

WITHIN 10 MINUTES we were pulling into the station's parking lot.

We both ran inside almost as soon as he put the car in park. The wind made the light rain whip into our faces, stinging like little ice pellets.

We passed the automatic doors, the empty receptionist desk, and found Larson standing by her desk, holding a metal tray.

"Those the puzzle pieces from the past two crime scenes?" Paxton asked.

She nodded as she started walking. "They're here. Lox already went down to evidence to get everything." She looked over her shoulder at us. "I don't know what you're expecting to find, but Chief said to help you in this investigation however we can."

Larson led us down the hallway to a heavyset metal door, past Chief Alvarado's office. On the right side of the door she typed a passcode on the keypad. A faint beep sounded along with an echoing click, and she opened the door and held it for us to follow behind her.

We entered a long room lined with several rows of metal shelves. The fluorescent lighting was sparse and some of the bulbs were flickering. Each of the shelves were filled with boxes of varying sizes.

"Lox?" Larson called out.

"Here." Lox's voice came from a few rows of shelves down. We followed it and found him standing at a table at the end of the row, looking down at an open box labeled *Holt, Delphina*. He had pulled out a couple of bags with different puzzle pieces and placed them on the table. One contained pieces from the puzzle that had been on the dining room table. The other contained the section of the puzzle we had seen on the floor in the corner of the picture. The red and blue pattern.

Larson placed the tray on the table beside the bags of puzzle pieces. Lox laid the bag down in the tray, the puzzle pieces inside still intact, and we all watched as he maneuvered all the pieces together into a perfect match.

Paxton swore. He took a few steps back and paced down the aisle, rubbing his hands through his hair. I set the case down at my feet and ran my fingers through my own hair. *Holy shit.*

Lox turned to look at us. "How did you know the puzzle pieces would match?"

"We didn't," I said. "Not for sure, anyway."

"But it was a damn good guess." Paxton walked back up the aisle.

"But what does this mean?" Larson asked.

I bent over the table, my arms supporting my weight. "It means... Jessie wasn't actually the first victim."

We all looked at each other in silence. The only noise present was the dim lights buzzing above our heads.

Paxton broke the silence first. "It means, my wife was the first victim."

Larson and Lox looked at Paxton in confusion, casting me quick glances.

I picked the briefcase up from the floor onto the table and unlatched it.

I gave a brief synopsis of the case, showing Larson and Lox the pictures.

"But what does that tell us in the long run?" Larson asked. "What do Jessie and Issie have to do with Delphina? Why the ten-year gap? How do we know they're truly related?"

"We don't still," I said. Lox studied the contents on the table and Paxton paced the small aisle close by. "But it can't be a coincidence that the puzzle pieces are a match."

All of us jumped at the sound of a phone ringing. Paxton's ringtone sounded. He and I exchanged quizzical looks as he pulled his phone out.

"Hello?" He furrowed his brow. "Delphi?"

"Wait, isn't she the one from the library?" Lox whispered to Larson.

"She's his niece," I whispered to them, my own brow furrowing. "But they spent all evening together."

"Delphi, I can't hear you so well, what's happ—" Every ounce of blood drained from his face. "Where are you?"

I couldn't make out her words, but her hysterical tone was piercing even from this far away. What could have happened in the few hours since she and Paxton spent time together?

He struggled to pull out his notebook, cursing as he dropped his pen and had to pick it up. "Say it again." He began writing. "Stay right there, do you understand? I'm on my way."

He hung up and look around at us, his eyes filling with tears and his expression filling with panic. "We have to go *now*. It's happened again. Callie, she's... she's..."

Lox raised his hand in a placating way. "She's *what*, man?"

"She's—" He let out a long breath. "Delphi found her. She's laying in a pool of blood like the others." Paxton stared ahead of him, his eyes unfocused. "Her eyes are gone."

The rest of us were stunned into silence.

Paxton looked at me and I saw his features harden. "We have to go. *Now!*"

"You go," Larson said. "I'll clean up here and follow."

Lox and Paxton ran to the doorway. I shoved the file papers back into the briefcase and started running. All the papers fell to the floor, descending like slow confetti, spreading out in every direction due to my momentum. In my urgency I hadn't thought to latch the case.

I cursed and quickly dropped to the ground to start gathering everything.

Paxton looked behind him and stopped in his tracks, about to say something before I cut him off first.

"Just go!" I said "I'll catch up!"

He nodded and ran out the door. Lox had held it open for him.

I cursed again, scrambling to get the papers picked up. *We do not have time for this.*

"You can ride with me," Larson said as she put the evidence box back onto the shelf.

"Thank you, I appreciat—" I caught sight of the picture in my hand. It was one I didn't recognize.

I frowned at it. I thought I had looked at every picture.

The photo was of Delphina and a young man who was not Paxton. Delphina looked younger in this picture, around the same age as her high school graduation photo. She was grinning, her arm around the boy next to her and she held up a puzzle box with her other hand. The boy was holding the box from the other side.

I looked at the picture closer. The boy was younger than Delphina, as if he was maybe a freshman or sophomore. He was skinny with the smallest wispy mustache growing at the corners of his mouth. His face was tilted slightly away from the camera, and he had only one side of his mouth upturned, as if he was deeply unhappy but knew he needed to smile for the camera.

He looked familiar. I was sure I had seen him before and recently. But where?

I turned the picture over and saw written there in neatly embellished handwriting:

Me + Rick. The puzzle I gave him when I left for college.

I turned the picture back over to look at the puzzle the two of them were holding. The picture was that of the San Francesco Bay Bridge against a bright blue sky.

Red lines against a bright blue backdrop. I blinked and looked away for a moment before turning my eyes back to it. Was I seeing this right? I looked at it again.

No. Yes. I was right.

This was the same puzzle we had just come here to check. The same puzzle that's been at every crime scene.

I looked up. "I need to talk to Tony."

Larson gave me an incredulous look, as she bent down to help gather the papers further down the aisle. "What? Dr. Grace, we gotta go—"

I slid the photo across the floor to her. "Look at the puzzle."

She picked it up and I saw her eyes widen. "You think—" She did the same double take I had to do. "But this could be anyone."

I kept scraping all the papers together in a messy pile. "Which is why I need to confirm it's not. Tony said there was another survivor. They have to be linked."

Larson tilted her head as she slid papers towards me. "But a kid?"

"He wouldn't be a kid anymore. That was about fourteen years ago. And he looks roughly fourteen in this picture."

Larson looked unconvinced.

"Please. This is the most solid lead we have. It's the *only* lead we have. We have to at least check."

She let out a breath that came out as a trill. "Fine. But we have to make it quick."

27 DEL

She was gone.

She was really and truly gone.

She wasn't coming back.

Mom. *Mom. Mom!*

I hit my dining room table with a closed fist, my mouth open in a silent scream. The back of my throat hurting from how much I was trying to prevent myself from melting into a puddle. Why hadn't I seen it?

She lived a few streets away from me, but I normally took a shortcut through the small woods between our places.

I liked taking evening walks. I usually would cut through the woods to her place, but I had decided to walk the long way around, so that I could stay on the sidewalk beside the well-lit street.

I had walked to her house to return some food containers. I had let myself in, expecting her to respond when I'd called her name but the house had been silent.

As I walked through, signs of struggle were clear all over the place. Her dining room chairs had been overturned. Water and shards of broken glass littered the floor. The remnants of a glass she had been drinking from. The back door was wide open.

Across from the door, the gate in the fence around her yard was also wide open. I saw imprints in her overgrown grass from the house through the gate. I called Mom's phone, startling when it started vibrating on the dining room table behind me.

That, more than anything else made me afraid. I pulled my taser out of my purse and followed the imprints in the grass. They led me down her private path into the woods.

And that's where I had found her.

I couldn't stomach the memory. I ran to the kitchen sink and dry heaved into it. Images from the crime scene flitted through my mind.

Blood.

Stab wound in the neck.

Empty eye sockets.

Wearing the same clothes she'd had on at the coffee shop.

That was the last time I had seen her. That was the last time I'd ever see her again.

I swore, wiping the line of saliva from my mouth. My arms were starting to buckle beneath my weight, my tensed muscles shaking. I sank down to the kitchen floor, shivering uncontrollably, and I tucked my arms around my knees.

I had called Uncle Ax. Told him to come right away. He had told me to stay there, but I didn't. I didn't listen. I couldn't. I couldn't stand to be next to her body.

I had run back to my house.

The kitchen was dark. My house was dark. I hadn't been able to muster the strength to turn the lights on.

I started rocking. I needed to call out of work tomorrow. Could I do that? Was that allowed?

My mother was just murdered. More than just murdered—she was mutilated. If I couldn't call out of work for *that*, then I would quit.

I took deep, calming breaths. My stomach gurgled. I wasn't sure if that was because there was nothing in it, or if it was from all the jitters coursing through my body. I certainly wasn't hungry.

Food. Why the hell was I even thinking about food right now?

My mom made good food. Last time she was here, she'd made a big pot of chili for me. I thought there was still some in the fridge.

The last meal she made me. That was the last meal she'd made me. I should freeze it, savor the last thing I would ever eat that was made by her. The thought had me biting my tongue to keep from crying out.

A funeral. I would have to organize a funeral. I've never done that before. I didn't know how. Was that something you could google? Who the hell do you invite to a funeral? She didn't have a lot of friends.

Dad. I would have to tell Dad. I was due to send him a letter soon. But he'd have to wait.

We didn't have a lot of family left either. All of my grandparents were dead. I had no aunts or uncles or cousins. Was there any point in a funeral then? She wouldn't have cared either way.

"Party or no party. As long as you're there, I'll be happy." That's what she'd told me at her last birthday. Gosh her last birthday. She had barely made it to her 40s.

I put my head on my knees. My whole body stopped shivering and went rigid. My mind felt like it was ballooning out, filling with so many thoughts and feelings. The utter inevitability of it all that my sanity was stretching thin, ready to burst with the smallest prick.

Ax.

I looked up at the thought. My uncle *was* back in Marlborough. That was something.

But I didn't know if I could rely on him to stay. I wasn't sure I wanted him to.

I didn't know what I wanted anymore. Everything felt pointless.

Click.

What was that?

I looked around. The kitchen had gotten darker, but my eyes had adjusted to the lack of light. It sounded like it had come from the hallway. Was it the front door?

A prickle ran across my back. Had I locked the front door?

I had always felt safe in my house. Marlborough had always been a safe place to live in the grand scheme of things. Was I crazy? I was sure I would be paranoid as all get out from now on. Maybe I should have listened to Ax—

A shadow flickered across the hallway.

I stood, cursing my creaky floors. With my left hand I pulled a knife from the knife block on the counter behind me and waited, wondering what I should do.

In horror movies, someone would call out, "Is anyone there?" And then they'd get slaughtered. I may not have ever been the smartest person in the room, but I sure as heck wasn't that stupid.

The shadow flickered again. This time, I thought I heard footsteps going into the living room.

My downstairs had a circular, old-fashioned layout where the front door opened to a hallway. Straight-ahead were the stairs that led to the second floor. To the left were the kitchen and dining room, and the living room to the right. I walked to the opposite end of my kitchen towards the entrance to the backyard and living room.

I stood still again, listening. My heart was pounding and all I could hear, all I could feel, was pressure in my ears. I took a deep silent breath, focusing as hard as I could.

But I heard nothing.

I lowered the knife. I *saw* nothing either.

The momentary relief vanished when a hand grabbed me around my throat from behind to my right.

I managed to turn slightly and bent my arm behind me, stabbing the knife backwards and hearing a grunt. The figure was taller than me by the sound of the now slightly labored breathing somewhere above my head.

I tried to push away, but the hand grabbed my throat tighter. I reached for the light-switch by the back door but only managed to turn the back door mudroom light on.

The stream of light cast long shadows in the kitchen. I managed to grab the handle of the knife and pull it up and out, causing my attacker to grunt in pain again. I tried to stab again, but the other hand grabbed my arm and dug its fingernails into the tendons of my wrist. The knife fell out of my hand and I cried out.

I tried stomping on my attacker's feet next, but he swept his leg under mine and I toppled backwards into his chest.

He let me drop to the floor, and I tried to scramble away but he jumped on top of me and straddled my chest, pinning my arms down with his legs. I looked up and saw his crotch, then his torso and then his face all in shadow as his back was to the light form the mudroom.

"Don't make me hit you," he said. "I don't want to spoil that pretty face of yours." He slid a finger down my cheek. I recoiled in disgust.

"Get *off* me." I grunted, his weight on my chest making it hard to talk. I flailed my feet around, but I couldn't reach him or anything else close to me.

His hands hovered over my face, like someone would hesitate to pick up a prized possession.

"What do you want with me?" I gasped, anger starting to flood my mind. "Why are you in my house?"

"The last puzzle piece."

"The last what?"

"Shhh. To sleep, beloved." He pressed a rag into my mouth.

I tried holding my breath, but the rag covered my nose and mouth and I was already winded from the struggle.

Where was my phone? Why hadn't I called 911 when I had the chance?

My last thought was of cameras and my mother's mutilated face before darkness consumed me.

28 WILLOW

Larson led me down a painted brick hallway to the two separate doors at the end. She stepped up to the left one and entered a code on another keypad on the right side of the door. A camera above the doors faced us.

Larson opened the door and inside was a small walkway to the holding cells. There were only two cells side by side in the Marlborough Police Department for male inmates. With each cell, three of the four walls were made of brick, while the final wall that opened onto the hall was lined with old-fashioned, white-painted bars. One was empty while Tony occupied the other.

"Dr. Vermont?" I said, approaching the bars. Larson stayed a few steps back.

Tony's cell was comprised of a square space with a steel cot along one wall and a metallic toilet and sink along another, all bolted to the floor.

Tony sat on his bed, reading a book. The covers were pulled up neatly, and his back was against the wall. He had looked up at the sound of us entering the holding area. As uncomfortable as it must have been, being here seemed to be doing him some good. His cheeks had filled out some since he had come in. He'd had a shower and the coveralls he was wearing were clean and devoid of holes. Even his beard and hair looked neater.

He sat up, his eyebrows raised. "Dr. Grace?"

I wrapped my fingers around the bars. "Three women have now died, and we need to know who did it. I understand it's hard to talk about, and I hate having to ask you to revisit these memories, but more lives are at stake. Please, will you help us? Will you help me?"

Tony's eyes bounced between the two of mine. I could see the cogs in his head turning, the hesitancy, the shame. He opened his mouth to speak but it seemed like he couldn't muster the words.

"We think we know who it is now, but I need you to confirm. All I need you to do is look at a picture and confirm if this is the other survivor." I pulled the picture out of my pocket and held it up, facing it away from him.

He hesitated a moment longer, staring at the picture in my hand.

Then he nodded. He stood up, laid the book open at his page, and limped up to the bars.

I handed him the picture. "Do you recognize the boy?"

Even if he had wanted to lie, he had no poker face. His lips tightened and his brow furrowed as he looked at the picture. His eyes glassed over.

"Yes. That's him."

I felt my heart begin to race and my face flush. "He's the other cult survivor? You're sure?"

Tony nodded, sniffing. "I helped him escape."

I glanced back at Larson and saw that she shared my understanding. I looked back at Tony. "What can you tell me about him?"

"His name is Derrick Landon, goes by Rick. He was born into the cult, knew nothing else until he was about fourteen." Tony swallowed. "You have to understand... these people were... different. They believed in a powerful deity of death, called the Bloodless One. They were trying to resurrect this god, piece by piece, by sacrificing body parts to him. They believed that, if the person who offered a part of their body lived, that was a sign he had accepted the sacrifice. But if the person died, it was a sign of his judgment, and they were unworthy."

This was not dissimilar to other blood cults I had read about. I nodded, prompting him to continue.

"Rick was different, even having been raised in the environment he was. He was reclusive and secretive. He loved puzzles. When I was brought into the flock, I made fast friends with him and his mother. She was kind to me. I took the boy under my wing and taught him things. I taught him how to skin and clean animals, to help his mother with the food prep as she was one of the cooks.

"Eventually his mother was selected as the Prayerful Bridge, a special larger kind of offering to the Bloodless One. She was required to offer a whole limb." Tony's mouth contorted, as if he was trying to hold back a sob. "She didn't survive."

My heart sank and stomach twisted.

"He wasn't supposed to be there. He wasn't supposed to see what happened to her. But he snuck in somehow and saw everything. He interrupted the ceremony, convinced that if they reattached her arm to her body, she would wake up. The leaders the... the Limbless Ones—the priests essentially—they would have killed him if I hadn't helped him escape."

Tony looked down at his bad foot. "They took my heel as punishment. They would have done more, but they needed to keep me relatively healthy if they wanted more of their own people to survive."

"You did what you had to do to survive."

"After... after everything happened I eventually saw him again. It was some years later, but that's how I knew he had survived. I was hunting in the woods one day, a few miles outside of Marlborough. It was well off the tracks, so you can imagine my surprise when I heard someone walking through the wet underbrush. He was older, but it was definitely him. He was wearing a sweatshirt with the local high school's mascot on it so I knew he must have found a place to land somehow. Over the years, I've seen him many times in the woods, and each time he looked angrier, always muttering to himself. I never stuck around long enough to observe anything more than if he was alive and relatively well fed."

I squeezed the bars before stepping back. "Thank you. Truly."

Tony took an uneven step back from the bars. I could see the pain morphing into anger as he squared his shoulders. "Now go do something about it."

Larson held the door open for me to leave the cell area. I gave Tony one last nod before walking through it.

"We have a suspect," Larson said. I could see hope igniting in her eyes. "Let's go see if he's in the database."

We made our way back to the main office. Larson ran to her computer and started typing before she had even sat down. I came up behind her to watch.

After a few seconds of furious typing, a picture filled the screen.

Gaunt face, greasy hair. He had been clean-shaven when we had seen him, but this picture showed him with a patchy beard and the skin around his mouth dry and spotty.

"That's the guy from the coffee shop," I said, surprised. "We saw him the other day in Cobain's. Nearly ran Paxton over on his way out of the bathroom."

Larson's eyes dashed back and forth across the screen, reading out loud. "Says here his name is Derrick Landon, age 30. Works for the Marlborough Local Forest Service, which is a program put together for adults who have a hard time holding down a regular job. Was the adoptive son of Jerry and Laura Smith, who have since moved from Marlborough back to Kentucky."

We both stared at his picture for a second, stunned. He was young, younger than me. And this is what he had chosen to do with his life?

Larson was the first to move, leaning back in her desk chair. "What could have caused him to go over the edge? I mean, serial killers don't usually go from zero to one hundred. Generally there's a build-up. But why dismember bodies?"

I thought back to what Tony had said. I started pacing between the desks. "It has to stem from his time in the cult..."

Larson nodded, turning back to the computer. "I'll see if I can pull up any more information about him. Maybe a car or an address."

I nodded, lost in thought.

The cultists believed in a deity they were trying to resurrect. They believed sacrificing body parts would bring this Bloodless One back from wherever he was. I thought about the remnants of those old books and the femur Paxton and I had found at the base of the mound, which I now knew for sure was an altar.

I stopped pacing. "I think he's trying to resurrect someone."

Larson snapped her head in my direction. "What?"

"That's the only thing that makes sense. But who would he want to resurrect?" I looked back down at the floor. "His mom? But then... how is Delphina connected to all of this?"

I picked the briefcase up and put it on the closest desk. I opened it and began flitting through the pages to see if I could find any more pictures of a younger Derrick Landon.

I found only one more picture with him in it, another picture from Delphina's going-away-to-college-party. It must have been taken in the same bout of pictures as the other picture of the two of them. They were still posing in the same positions, both sitting and holding the puzzle between them, but Delphina and Derrick had moved slightly. Delphina had been caught mid laugh and Derrick looked directly at her.

He hadn't been smiling before, but now he had a grin on his face as he watched Delphina laugh. A grin and a gleam in his eye.

It was hungry. As if he couldn't get enough of her.

The vibration of my phone startled me so much I dropped the picture on the floor. I answered the phone, bending over as I did to retrieve the picture.

"Paxton?"

Paxton's voice was frantic. "Delphi was right," he said, his voice wet. "Callie's dead and—and—damn it. Her eyes are gone, Willow, just like she said. There's a section of that damn puzzle on her chest. And I can't find Delphi. She's not here and she's not answering her phone. I'm headed to her house now."

I felt my stomach drop. "Paxton, we have a suspect."

Larson glanced at me, nodding.

Paxton's heavy breathing filled the other end of the line. "Who?"

I explained everything that Tony had just told me. "Delphina is connected somehow. I think—" I stopped, my mouth going dry. "I think he's trying to resurrect Delphina."

29 HOLT

Derrick Landon.

After all these years, did I finally know the name of my wife's killer? *Delphi. Delphina.*

My niece's and wife's faces kept flashing back and forth across my mind with each breath I took as I ran. My breathing became more ragged the faster I ran. This couldn't happen. Not again. Not to my niece, my only connection left to Delphina.

I told Lox where I was going but he'd only acknowledged me with a nod as he called for backup. I ran from the crime scene—*Callie's* crime scene— towards my niece's house, having glanced at the map to her house on my phone before starting.

I cut through the woods, trying and failing to keep fear and suspicion at bay. I tried to focus on the sound of the leaves and twigs crunching under each footfall, the flashlight from my phone illuminating the path in front of me, hell even my breathing. But questions kept tumbling in my mind.

Why hadn't she answered her phone? Was the same person behind all of this? The same person who had killed her, my Delphina, all those years ago?

Resurrect my wife? *My* wife? Why?

And how?

And where the hell was Delphi?

I hoped she was home. But if any of my suspicions were confirmed—

I couldn't think like that. Not right now. She was home, and I was almost there. She *had* to be there.

Marlborough had a couple of neighborhoods, but they were all small and spread out, thick pockets of forest separating all the clusters of houses. I started to taste copper on my tongue as the side of a two-story house came into view. I slowed my pace, trying to gain control of my erratic breathing and heartrate.

I ran up to the front door and started hammering on it with my fist as loud as I could. "Del? It's me. It's Ax. Del, can you let me in?"

But as I hit the door it pushed ajar. Why would it have been left open like this? It was a safe enough town but under the circumstances, Delphi wouldn't have left it like this. I didn't blame her for not staying when I told her to—no one could stomach seeing their mother mutilated. But the lights here weren't even on.

And the door was now wide open.

I pulled my gun from its holster and held it at a low ready as I made my way inside.

Straight ahead was the stairwell. To the right was the walkway into the living room. To the left was the walkway into the kitchen.

No immediate lights shone anywhere I could see.

"Del?"

I felt around and turned on the light to the living room, staying at the ready. There was a small love seat and an armchair with a small side table in between. A framed painting was on the wall above a small fireplace. A few bookshelves stuffed with books framed the fireplace.

Nothing looked amiss. Further along the wall I had come through was another doorway. I walked towards it, noticing a light was on there, and came to a mud room of sorts. It was much smaller than the entryway by the front door, large enough only to open the back door and take one's shoes off.

I passed through the mudroom and looked through the doorway on the other side.

A chair was overturned with a jacket splayed out under it.

I turned the light on, exposing the remnants of a small commotion that had taken place in the kitchen.

The sink, stove, and small counter space lined one wall. On the other side was a small table. One seat was pushed in neatly, while the other was on its side. There were small splatters of blood on the checkered linoleum, and I saw a bloodied knife on the floor in the corner of the room. I glanced at the counter and saw one of the slots in the knife block was empty.

Something on the dining room table caught my eye. I moved in closer, still holding my gun at the ready. My stomach sank to my feet.

The final corner of that damned puzzle.

I darted through the kitchen and up the stairs, calling for Del, but the house was silent and empty.

Like I knew in my gut it would be as soon as I saw those pieces.

I came back down the stairs, holstering my gun, and I stopped in the kitchen entrance again. *No, no, no. Not again. Please, not again.*

I swore, hitting the door frame with the side of my fist. I ran my hand through my hair, trying to remain calm.

I tried calling Del again.

I heard a faint buzzing from the floor in the kitchen. I looked at the jacket under the chair and approached it, digging through the pockets until I found her phone. I pulled it out and saw the words *Uncle Ax* written on the top of the screen over a picture of the two of us when she was little.

My contact information was already logged into her phone.

My heart swelled and broke all at once. I clenched my jaw to keep the hurt at bay. I had walked away from her once. I would never do so again.

I hung up my call and dialed Willow. She answered on the second ring.

"Paxton?"

"She's not here." I looked around the kitchen again, noting all the evidence. "She's not at her house but she might have been attacked. There's some blood splatter on the floor along with a bloodied knife. She must have been here recently—I found her phone in a jacket and the outside of the jacket's wet. Guessing this is what she was wearing when she found her m— Callie." I began pacing, doing everything I could to keep the panic rising in me at bay.

Willow cursed.

A weight of inevitability began to crash down on me. "That's not all. I found another section of that puzzle left on her dining room table. Willow, I don't know what to do. If she's not already dead, there's no knowing where she could be."

"We're going to figure it out. He's changed up his pattern. He killed and then immediately went after another victim. There has to be a reason."

I threw my hands up. "But what, *what* could be the reason? And why Delphi?"

A sigh sounded through her end. I could imagine her eyebrows scrunching together the way she normally does when she's thinking. "Let's look at this from the resurrection approach. Tony told us the cult would take human body parts in hopes of resurrecting their deity, right?" I nodded before I realized she couldn't see me. She continued anyway. "Well, Derrick Landon has already taken two arms, two legs, and a set of eyes. All that remains to build a body is the torso and—"

"The head." I stopped pacing. "Willow, Delphi looks exactly like Delphina, aside from her eyes. But Callie's eyes looked exactly like hers. Once he got the eyes, he realized Del was his missing final piece." My mouth went dry. "This is insane, but you might be right. He's trying to Frankenstein Delphina back together. But why? He can't possibly believe that he's actually going to bring her back from the dead."

"I went through Delphina's file again and I found another picture of the two of them. I think... I think Derrick might have been in love with her."

Bile rose up my throat. "What?"

"Seems like they were in high school together, though he was a bit younger than her. Maybe, after everything that happened to his mom and then his escape from the cult, the trauma caused him to latch onto someone. From everything I've heard about Delphina, it's not unreasonable to think she would have been kind to him."

I shook my head. "He didn't just latch onto her. He was *obsessed* with her." Tears pricked my eyes as I looked around my niece's kitchen. But the truth left my mouth before I could stop myself. "She was right. The whole time we'd lived here together, she was being stalked. If I had just taken her fears seriously and really listened..."

"Listen to me," Willow said, her tone as gentle as a feather. "This was not your fault. If you really want to argue about that later, we can, but you were young and newly married. You did your best with what you had at the time.

But right now, we don't have time to try and fix the past. We have to find your niece. Larson is still looking to see if we can find anything else out about Derrick, a car, an address, anything."

My other hand began to vibrate and I realized I still gripped Delphi's phone as though it were a lifeline. I looked at it, the bright glow of the screen shining in the dark kitchen, and saw a notification from Instagram. Underneath it was a notification from an app called Home Security which said *Movement Recorded.*

There was a small picture on the right part of the notification. Squinting at it, I realized it was me. I scrolled through her notifications and saw several more from Home Security.

The lightbulb was instantaneous.

"Willow, I might have found something." I put my phone between my shoulder and ear so that I could use both hands on Del's.

"What do you have?"

"It looks like she had a camera set up by her front door and it's connected to an app on her phone." I chuckled in spite of myself. "Smart girl. She's like you; lived alone and knew she needed some protection." I thought back to when we'd met Del in the Marlborough PD parking lot. I thought about the pattern her thumb had made over her screen to unlock it.

I mimicked the pattern and her phone opened. I released a fast exhale, adrenaline beginning to pump through me again. I searched for the Home Security app and found it before I'd typed in the full name. Clicking on it allowed me complete access to her security footage. Different recordings had been taken today, each listed with a thumbnail image and a timestamp. I scrolled past the ones that were surely me and the time that I came here. The last recorded were from just a few minutes ago. I clicked on the one before it. The thumbnail showed it was brighter outside, and Delphi was outside her door. I clicked on it.

"Looking at the footage now," I told Willow.

The camera must have been hidden under the rain gutters. The image was tilted down from the right side of the front door. There was a decent view of the street in front of the house, though the image was bowed along the edge of screen, like when you look through a peephole.

I watched Del leave the house, closing the front door and locking it behind her. It was still light outside, and she walked out of sight to the right, holding a couple of plastic food containers in her hands. This was probably when she'd left to go to her mom's. At the coffee shop earlier, they'd talked about meeting up at Callie's house in the evening so Del could return some food containers. Callie had talked about making dinner and invited me to come along, but I'd declined.

Now I wished I hadn't.

The next recording took place about forty-five minutes later. It was darker in this recording, so I couldn't make out Del's face until she ran right up to the front door, tears streaming down her face. This had to be when she'd run back here to escape seeing her mother mutilated like that. I clicked on it.

I filled Willow in.

"Is there anything else after that?" she asked.

The next recording showed a car driving up to the house and parking backwards in the driveway, the movement triggering a motion sensitive light. I could not make out many details of the vehicle from the angle it had parked.

"A car just pulled in."

"Did you happen to see a license plate?"

"The car's too far from the camera to make out the license plate right now. Hold on."

A figure got out of the car and marched up to the door. I couldn't see his face, but the lanky build and jerky movements told me this was a man. He kept his head down, a bag over his shoulder, with plastic booties over his shoes and latex gloves on his hands. Smart man. He knew he wasn't safe. Any trace of his DNA left behind would start the most voracious hunt of my career. Yet he didn't look up and notice the security cameras. When he let himself into the house the recording ended.

The next began about ten minutes later when the man opened the front door, carrying Del's limp body over his shoulder. I couldn't see any blood from the angle, but it was hard to tell with the pixilation worsening with the growing darkness. He shut the door behind him and walked towards his car, popping the trunk open as he came closer. The automatic light turned on again but the details were getting harder and harder to make out. He turned to place her in the trunk and I could see her hands bound together, and it looked like her mouth was taped shut. He dropped her into the trunk, and closed it, not even bothering to look around and see if he was spotted before getting into the driver's seat and driving away.

I gave Willow a play-by-play, rewinding the video and rewatching it to make sure I had every detail right.

Willow cursed under her breath. "How did the neighbors not see him?"

"Del doesn't have any close neighbors. She lives down a drive by herself," I replied.

I clicked the recording, showing the car backing into her driveway. I took a screenshot of the frame and viewed it in Del's camera role.

I zoomed in on the plate. A surge of adrenaline coursed through when I was able to make out a few of the digits. "I've got a partial plate." I read what I could see to Willow.

Rapid keyboard clacking sounded in the background and I waited, clenching my jaw. "We have a match."

"Have Larson see if she can find a match on any of the street cameras in Marlborough."

I backed out of the picture on the screen, about to close the phone when a picture a little bit down her camera roll caught my attention.

When I didn't respond, Willow called my name. "Paxton?"

"Hold on."

I clicked on it, and a picture of a car in front of a house came into place.

My house. My old house that Delphina and I had shared together.

The house she had been murdered in.

The picture had been taken from across the street a ways down, but even with the distance I could see the front lawn was entirely overgrown. It was strange seeing it again after all these years, like seeing the tombstone of a family friend. A wave of painful nostalgia surged through me before I shook my head, refocusing. I zoomed in on the car in the driveway. The same car from the recordings. I zoomed in on the license plate and saw the same letters I had just read off to Willow. In this one, I could read the full plate.

I clicked the details of the picture and saw it had been taken last week. Several contacts came up as suggestions to send the picture to. Above the contact title *Mom* was a call-to-action, saying *Send again*.

Clicking on it brought me to Callie and Del's text conversation. I scrolled up a ways and found Del had sent the picture along with a text that read:

. . .

Do you know if someone bought Uncle Ax and Aunt Delphina's house? I was on my morning run and I passed by and saw this.

Callie had replied:

    I don't think so. As far as I know, Ax still owns the property. Weird though, maybe it's getting maintenance done?

Why does he still own it? Seems like a waste of money?

I don't blame him, sweetie. I mean, that was the last place she was alive.

Holy shit.

    "Paxton?"

    "Willow... I think I know where he's taken Del."

30 THE KILLER

I'M NOT CRAZY.

It was all too easy.

I placed the soon-to-be face of my beloved into position on the altar I had erected over the exact spot she had died. The kitchen had long since been wiped clean of her blood since that day ten years ago. But I remembered it as though it were yesterday. In fact, every time I looked at the floor, I could see it as though it were still happening right in front of me. And this girl, this precious one who looked so much like my love, was still unconscious. On top of the very spot Delphina had died, I envisioned blood spilling onto the floor once more. Soon, I wouldn't have to imagine anymore.

Soon, this girl would never be conscious again.

I'm not crazy.

Others like me have said before that it's easier to kill than one would expect. I found that they were right. It is easy to pick the sacrifice, to wield the knife, to catch them unawares. It is easy to do each step.

But to watch the life leave their eyes? To watch their lungs deflate as their last breath leaves their body?

That was not hard, nor was it easy.

That was a privilege.

It was an honor to witness. One that I was grateful to behold, more than I could express.

If they only knew what they had given their lives to, such a beautiful cause. Anyone would—*should*—be honored to give their life to another.

Especially to her.

Delphina.

My sweet Delphina.

I'm not crazy.

All these long years, I had lived without her, in a world devoid of her radiance. I had thought about ending it all. I had even tried to. At least then I may have a chance to be with her but...in the end, I decided it was my penance to endure the world without her. Since it was my fault she had died.

My fault for pushing her. My fault for being a coward all those years ago. If only I had voiced my love for her sooner. If only I could have shown her the depths of my love for her. If only she could have seen how she had made me feel a safety I hadn't felt since my mother's last caress.

If she had only listened to me. She hadn't understood how important she was to me.

I hadn't meant to snap.

She was just close to me—closer than we'd been in years—and the next thing I knew, she was on the floor, drenched in blood.

This floor, this very floor that I was now standing on.

I'm not crazy.

I had not been idle, all these years since she had died. I had done research. Research on what it takes to bring back the dead. I had gone back to where my mother had died, searching for the tomes the Limbless Ones had safeguarded that explained the resurrection rituals. Time and the elements had destroyed the Temple, but I had found one book still intact at the base of the altar.

Yet with all their precious rule keeping and rituals performed to perfection, the Limbless Ones had been monsters, worshiping a false god. They had murdered my mother for nothing. They had completed their sacrifice to resurrect The Bloodless One, and yet he had not shown up. And I knew then that the Bloodless One's reign could not lead to truth. My mother being chosen as the Prayerful Bridge had been an absolute waste.

They'd said her death was a clear indication of the Bloodless One's displeasure, that his blessing would be proven by her surviving the sacrifice. My mother had been perfect—why else would they have chosen her? Clearly, the Bloodless One must have been wrong.

Or non-existent.

I'm not crazy.

The Limbless Ones had one thing right—it takes the ultimate sacrifice for the dead to rise. I would not be performing the resurrection ritual out of fear in order to bring back a blood-thirsty false god. I would be performing it for the betterment of the world. My world. With sacrificial gifts, not bloody penance owed.

Gifts. What those women provided were gifts, though they did not know it.

Like Calliope. If she had known that her death would be used for a greater purpose, for the return of a world with Delphina in it, she would have given it willingly.

She just hadn't known how.

So I'd shown her.

I'm not crazy.

Each piece of Delphina had been carefully chosen from others of similar builds and heights to Delphina. They would do nicely, so very nicely.

Her eyes had been unique. A hue only she and her sister had shared.

With those special puzzle pieces, the limbs, Callie's eyes, and Delphi's face and torso... the greatest puzzle I had ever put together would be complete.

The final piece, the girl, had been one I'd had my eye on for a while. I had given Delphi Augur no thought at all until I saw her at the library.

It wasn't long after I'd decided to bring Delphina back into the world again. I had already spent months researching methods and means. I spent much time in the forest to gather my pieces. And lucky for me, they had obliged. It was as if they'd known the importance of my mission all along.

I just hadn't had her face. The most important puzzle piece of all.

On that fateful day, I had been walking in the forest and had come up the trail behind the library. I hadn't planned on going in. I merely was skirting around the building to get back to my car, but I saw someone through the window.

She had been standing next to a cart, shelving books. I had thought it was Delphina at first glance, the girl looked so much like my love.

But she had turned. Her face was a near perfect replica of Delphina, aside from her eyes. I stood there admiring her as she put the books away, getting a thrill every time she bent over or reached for a higher shelf, revealing creamy, perfect skin.

My research had begun anew.

I had discovered the woman I had seen was Delphi Augur, Delphina's niece. I hadn't considered the rest of Delphina's family for years. But now I saw the powers that be had handed me the final piece to this puzzle on a silver platter. The powers that be, like a voice inside my head, pushing me down this path to Delphina. *I'm not crazy.*

I watched her as I had the others, learning her routine. It had been a privilege.

As had assembling the puzzle pieces.

I had saved the other pieces in freezers I had found, small ones that could be run off generators. I knew that I would need to be able to preserve them, especially if the right opportunity to take action did not present itself on schedule.

I looked down at the girl on the altar and felt my heart melt. I ran a finger over her forehead, brushing her lovely hair out of her face. She was so sweet and innocent. Perfect. Beautiful. Delectable.

The girl moaned softly, the smallest slits in her eyes opening as her head lulled to one side.

She was awakening.

I made sure Delphina's face was secure, tying her tightly to the altar with rope. I reveled in the sound of her soft moans as I tied her in place. I rubbed my side, feeling where she had stabbed me. This pain would be the last of my penance.

Tonight would be the night.

Tonight, I would see my Delphina again.

I am not crazy.

31 WILLOW

The house looked eerie in the light of the moon and a single lamppost.

It had stopped raining and the night sky was clear. The ground around the lamppost was still wet, its reflection glittering against the pavement.

Even in the dark, it was clear the house had long since been abandoned. The lawn was overgrown, the weeds vining up between the cracks and breaks in the cement driveway. A car was parked all the way up the drive, far enough back from the streetlight that I hadn't seen it until we'd driven up and parked off the road.

The house had no near neighbors, but wasn't too far from a main road and sidewalk.

I tried to imagine Paxton and Delphina here, playing with a little Del in the front yard and Callie watching them close by, all a happy little family. But the weight of the matter at hand was too overwhelming to even conjure that happy, homely scene for very long.

Paxton had left the PD with Deputy Lox in a police cruiser, so I went to pick him up from Del's house. Larson had stayed to put together a team and inform Chief Alvarado, who was en route from Seattle, of everything that had transpired tonight. As I drove us here, Paxton had also called Chief Alvarado to tell him what we were going to do. He had encouraged us to wait for backup.

As we watched the house, we saw a flickering light through some blinds on one of the bigger windows.

"They'll be here soon," I said to Paxton, turning to look at him in the passenger seat.

He nodded, his face rigid as he kept his eyes on the house. "We don't have time to wait for them. Even if we did, I'm not going to." His hand rested on the doorhandle, waiting for a cue to go.

I looked back at the house. "I didn't think you would."

As we watched, the light behind the blinds kept getting brighter.

"Do you think he's lighting a fire?" I asked, pulling a flashlight from my purse and putting it in my coat pocket.

"The light looks like it's coming from multiple sources. Maybe candles?" Paxton leaned forward, squinting. "Regardless, he's in the living room. We should walk around the back of the house and enter from the back door. By the time we nab him, the backup will be here. He won't have any place to run if we block him in."

"What if he's armed?" I asked.

Paxton turned and looked at me, placing a hand against his covered holster. That was response enough. "Let me handle him. I want you to get Del."

I nodded.

"Let's go get her." He began opening the passenger door, but I put my hand on his arm.

"Whatever happens in there..." I struggled to get the words out, knowing time was of the essence. "You're not in this alone. I'm here. And... I love you." I felt a swoop in my stomach as I said the words. I had referenced loving him before, but I had never outright said it.

Paxton's stared at me with the most intense gaze. He leaned across the console, grabbed the back of my head, and kissed me hard. I could feel the intensity behind this kiss, as if he was trying to convey more to me than words could say.

He broke away and got out of the car without another word.

I watched as Paxton pulled his Glock from the holster he had under his arm and held it at a low ready. He jerked his head for me to follow behind him and we started running as quietly as we could up to the house, staying low and just outside of the light from the lamppost. The moon shone in slivers through the trees, but the forest around the house was so thick, it didn't provide us much light to see by.

Paxton led us around to the back. The grass was wet and mushy, making a *shluc* sound with every step we took. One of my feet slipped in a gopher hole in the ground, nearly knocking me over on hands and knees before I caught myself. Cold wetness seeped inside of my sock and I yanked my foot out of the hole. Paxton hadn't stopped, continuing to the house. I pulled my foot out of the muck and rushed back up behind him.

We came up to the back door, a step between the base of it and the ground. Holt tried opening it. The handle wouldn't budge

"How are we going to get in?" I whispered.

Paxton looked through the window on the back door. "Hold on." He stepped back from the door but kept one foot on the step. He wiggled it and the step moved, the cement clicking against itself. I cupped the end of the flashlight and turned it on, holding the muted light over the step.

He stepped off and holstered his gun, then tilted the step up. The whole thing lifted off the ground like pulling off the top off a teapot. Underneath was a little cubby.

"She was always losing her keys, so I made sure she had a backup, just in case."

The corners of my mouth turned up at that, hiding a hint of a smile from Paxton as continued his task.

Paxton pulled a key from inside a plastic container that was tucked away in the corner. Inside the container was also a sheathed knife. He gripped its handle and faced the blade towards him to hand it to me.

"Just in case. Aim for any place soft, like the neck, armpit, or lower torso."

I took the knife and nodded, handing him the light. I hooked the sheath to my belt, then tested pulling the knife out. It popped out seamlessly. Images of the girls at the crime scenes flashed through my mind and I felt a mix of nausea and resolution. I put it back and nodded to Paxton, taking the flashlight back.

I had done what needed to be done before. I would do so again

He lowered the step back into place and pulled his gun back out of its holster. He stepped up to the door, silently unlocking it and pushing it open.

We both tensed as a small squeak sounded. The door opened into a spacious laundry room. I could see the hookups for the washer and dryer on the right wall, not attached to any appliances.

We walked forward, our feet making a light crunching sound on the dusty floor. The air smelled musty, and the room was filled with the sound of low humming. I held my flashlight up.

Two deep freezers were squeezed into the room. A sour, tangy smell filled the room. Paxton and I exchanged puzzled looks.

"Why are these here?" I whispered aloud.

"And what are they running on?" Paxton whispered back, but that was answered by my flashing my light behind one of the freezers. A portable generator was on the floor along the wall. Two cords were plugged into it, each leading back to a freezer.

My hands started to sweat as I realized what could be inside them. I held my flashlight up and opened the freezer closest to me.

I let out a gasp and almost let the lid slam shut before catching it. My eyes filled with tears as I bit my lip to keep from making a sound.

Paxton opened the other freezer and shut it just as quickly. He bit his lip, took a deep breath then gave me a look that said without words *"It's okay, it's okay."*

Two frozen solid human arms lay in the bottom of the freezer I had opened. In addition, there was a small clear plastic container that held two eyeballs laying on top of one of the hands.

My stomach writhed.

Paxton swallowed and shut his eyes tight. After a deep breath, he nodded towards a doorway. I nodded back and cupped the light again.

We walked together down a short hallway. The ground was still gritty with dust. Had no one lived here since Delphina had died? The walls were illuminated with flickering light, but it was enough for me to turn the flashlight off.

The hallway opened into a large room and I recognized the space from the pictures in Delphina's file. On the other side of the large room was a short hallway that I guessed led to the master bedroom. On the left wall was the front door. Off the right wall was the large open kitchen. We walked towards it and I expected the dining room table from the pictures in the file. But it was gone.

In the middle of the space dividing the kitchen from the living area room was Del, laying on top of a makeshift altar, surrounded by a white chalk or salt circle lined with many fat, dripping candles.

Paxton and I both ran to her.

Her eyes were wide open and when she saw us, she let out a closed mouth sob and tears spilled down the side of her eyes into her hair. Her mouth was covered in duct tape, and her chest rose and fell rapidly. Blood stains splotched her torso. She was tied in place by a rope, all her limbs spread like a starfish. More rope was tied around her shoulder and hip sockets, but so tightly her limbs were turning purple.

"We're going to get you out." Paxton peeled the tape from her mouth while I pulled my knife out and started cutting the rope around her extremities.

She swore as the tape tore from her skin. "I don't know where he went," she said, sobbing. "Last thing I remember was him knocking me out at my house, and the next thing I knew, I woke up here." She swore as I cut away the cords around her left shoulder.

"Is that your blood?" I asked, nodding to her torso as I worked at the rope.

"It's his. I stabbed him before he knocked me out. I don't know if it did any real damage," Del said. "I wish I could have done more, but he had tied me so tightly I couldn't move, and the tape was over my mouth. I was so groggy from whatever he drugged me with when I finally came to, I didn't even try to fight him"—She swore again as I cut through the ropes around her left hip—"as he got me onto this and tied me down."

"It's gonna be okay," Paxton said. "Backup is on their way. Del, I'm so sorry—"

"What do you think you're doing?" A calm voice said. The words were spoken at a normal volume but sounded like a scream in the silence.

All three of us looked around. Paxton whipped out his gun.

A man in white robes held a knife about ten feet away.

32 THE KILLER

It was the sweetest kind of torture, standing in the master bedroom of her house.

The furniture was long gone, but I could remember how their room had been set up. I remembered the dresser she had inherited from her parents, the small side tables she had found at a garage sale. She'd loved sitting at her vanity under the window, brushing her long, beautiful hair.

Watching her get dressed in the morning was my ultimate delight. After she brushed her hair, she would then rub lotion onto her face, neck, shoulders, and breasts.

I felt my body react to the memory.

I inhaled, trying to smell the room as it once had been, but I couldn't smell anything. I walked over to where her vanity had been and took another deep breath. Still nothing. Looking around the room, my eyes rested on the indents in the carpet where their bed had rested. I certainly didn't want to remember where she'd spent the nights with *him*. I looked down at my feet.

Wait. The carpet.

I got down on my hands and knees and smelled the carpet.

There, I could smell her. So faintly.

I stayed there for a minute, enjoying the vestiges of her perfection, the remnants of her body occupying this space. How often she looked so content sitting at her vanity, the smile on her face my joy and my agony. Knowing she was happy but not with me. Knowing she soon would be with me again.

Again, my body reacted.

Soon, she would be back in the world again. They say love conquers all. In this case, my love for her would conquer the grave.

The Bloodless One be damned.

The Limbless Ones be damned.

I thought of the women who had sacrificed their lives and limbs for Delphina, and I blessed their names, one by one. Their deaths had been for the greater good, I wanted them to know that. I hoped they knew that, wherever they were. They had to know that this woman was the embodiment of perfection, and her resurrection was worth all of humanity's demise.

But I didn't need *that* many pieces to complete my prized puzzle.

I thought of my mother. She had sacrificed her life to be the Prayerful Bridge. I, too, had made sacrifices—only my sacrifice wouldn't be in vain. The sheer force of my will, my love, my worship of Delphina's perfection would grant me success where my mother's sacrifice had failed.

The final piece to my puzzle was in the other room, over the exact place my Delphina had died. That would be where she would return to the world. That was important. The Limbless Ones had taught me that—they had been good for something. Location, proximity, will power, and an emotion so fierce it could conquer death were needed. The Limbless One's mistake had been letting fear be their emotion instead of true devotion.

Tonight would be the night. Tonight was the night the world would be graced with Delphina Augur—not Holt— again.

Even in my head I choked on that other surname, his taint the only mar to her perfection.

Holt. *Holt.*

I'd spent most of my time ignoring his existence. *I* was barely worthy of her, but him? Agent Paxton Holt? He did not deserve to even kiss the soles of her feet after she had walked through a freshly manured field. He must have duped her to get her wrapped around his thumb, and that was no way to win someone's affection. She'd just never realized the mistake she had made.

I had been so sure she would have realized her mistake when I had come to her that day, all those years ago. I hadn't explained myself properly. And she had ended up dead because of it.

How I look forward to seeing Holt's face when he sees what I am going to do. He will then understand an iota of the pain I have endured, the fool.

Still on hands and knees, my face pressed against the floor, I inhaled her scent again, that smell of summer flowers mixed with the rain. Deep relief coursed through my whole body, relaxing me.

I stood and winced. My side stung with the recent wound and I clutched it with a hand, then pulled it away. Shining blood stained my palm and fingers. If I touched the wall, it would make a perfect print. My knife wound still oozed, but the bleeding had slowed. A worthy price to pay, no matter the inconvenience. The final puzzle piece had gumption, same as Delphina did.

Delphina would be pleased with the body she would be resurrected into. I had chosen every piece to make an exact replica. I knew her proportions to a T, even all these years later I could remember every inch of her like she was right in front of me. These women, my sacrifices, were meant to be made into my beloved.

I donned my robes I had gotten especially for the occasion and strapped the ritual knife to my hip. I took it out of its sheath, admiring it. After the Limbless Ones had been arrested all those years ago and I had found out we had been close to Marlborough all this time, I'd returned to the forest. I'd searched until I finally found one of the ritual knives buried in the underbrush along with one of the ancient texts that told me everything I needed to know about sacrifices and resurrection.

How fitting that such a weapon would be used to bring back good into this world rather than cause more pain. My head snapped up when I heard low murmuring coming from the other room.

I opened the master bedroom door quietly and slipped out, keeping the unsheathed knife in my hand. The resurrection altar came into view. Delphina's final puzzle piece was still there. So were Agent Paxton Holt and Dr. Willow Grace on either side of the her, cutting the cords I had so carefully wrapped around her.

I had known they were on my trail. I knew if they had any brains at all they would have eventually connected the puzzle pieces to me.

I had not anticipated they would make the connection so quickly.

"Is that your blood?" Dr. Grace asked my final piece, working at the rope around the girl's shoulder.

The Limbless Ones had flown into a rage when I had interrupted their ritual. Now these people were interrupting mine, but I would not be so reckless and brash. I needed to think how to best stop them.

"It's gonna be okay," I heard Holt whisper. "Backup is on their way. Del, I'm so sorry—"

I took a step forward, out of the shadows, and raised the knife.

Ready to face those on my trail at last.

"What do you think you are doing?" My voice came out calm and collected.

All three of them looked around to me. Holt pulled his gun from his holster.

"Do you have any idea how important a ritual you're interrupting?" I asked, my voice still calm. I would speak to them like children, try to get them to understand. "Do you dare to prevent that which must occur?"

Holt looked round at Del before looking back at me. "Yes. We do."

"Foolish. This is for the good of us all."

"What possible good can come from murdering and dismembering three women?" Holt asked me. "For abducting another with clear intention of further harm?" The candlelight flickered around his face, causing him to look ghoulish.

That's exactly what he was. A ghoul. A monster.

"From ashes comes beauty," I replied. "Sacrifice is needed for perfection to re-enter the world."

"Can you tell us why?" Dr. Grace asked. "What—who are you trying to help re-enter the world?" She had walked around the altar to Holt's other side, her hands empty and raised.

Finally, someone asked an intelligent question.

"The embodiment of perfection, Dr. Grace—yes, I know who you are." I said, seeing the look of surprise on her face. "You're a survivor, just like me. I saw you on TV from that kidnapped heiress case you solved. If anyone would understand the importance of bringing beauty back into the world, it's you."

Dr. Grace nodded. "It's true, I am a survivor. So help me understand."

I put my hand to my side. My hand still gripped the knife but I no longer needed to threaten them. I was pleased by her inquisitiveness. "Nothing in my life made sense," I said. "That's why I like puzzles. From chaos comes order. She... she was that for me."

"She?" Dr. Grace asked. I watched her glance at Holt and felt a jolt of anger crackle through me like lightning. Would everyone turn their attention to him, leaving me?

"Yes, *she!*" The anger colored my words as I spat them aloud. "The love of my life. Delphina."

Holt shifted his weight, still pointing his gun at me. "Do you mean, Delphina *Holt?* My wife?"

It was becoming difficult to remain calm. My chest began to constrict, my grip on the knife becoming painfully tight. "She should never have married you. It was her only mistake in life. But you were bad for her, Holt. You couldn't even save her."

I took enormous satisfaction in seeing pain flash over his face. "By the sacrifice of others, she shall be resurrected into this world, puzzled back together."

"You're crazy. You can't bring people back from the dead. Delphina would be appalled by what you've done."

"I am not crazy!" I yelled, starting to boil over. "Delphina will *thank* me. She will—"

Sirens.

All of us paused as the high-pitched noise got louder and louder. Rage and panic exploded in me.

No, no, no!

I threw my knife at Holt and ran.

33 HOLT

I PUSHED Willow out of the way, both of us landing on the floor. The knife clattered behind us. He ran past us and I shot at his retreating back from the ground, aiming to debilitate.

He kept running, making it to the laundry room.

I looked at Willow, hesitating.

"I have her!" she said. "Go!"

I scrambled up to my feet and ran.

The back door Willow and I had come through was wide open. I saw his back as he ran towards the woods that made up the back part of the property.

I ran after him.

The trees were spread further apart here and the ground was more even. I was able to keep my sights on him as he ran, even in the dark. The minimal light of the moon that filtered through the branches and allowed me some semblance of vision.

I lost sight of him when he darted behind a tree.

I stopped, my lungs on fire as I tried to quiet my breathing. "You were there when my wife died all those years ago, weren't you?" I called out to him. "Was it you who pushed her?"

All I could hear was the blood pounding through my ears.

I took a few tentative steps forward and a figure ahead began running. I shot after him and resumed my chase.

The ground began to get steeper as I moved further into the tree line.

I could hear him panting, his steps slowing as he held a hand on his side. Despite the darkness, I could tell the stain I had seen on his side earlier had gotten bigger. A stark contrast to the white of his robes.

"Freeze!" I yelled.

He slowed.

"Freeze or I'll shoot!"

He stopped and turned back to me. His hand was still clutched to his side and I could tell he was as out of breath as I was. "Delphina deserved better than you!"

"You think she deserved someone like you?" I said, my gun still at the ready as I walked closer to him. "The man who murdered innocent women, including her sister? The man who kidnapped her niece?"

"If they knew who they were sacrificing themselves for, they would gladly present anything they could give."

"Then why didn't you sacrifice yourself?"

His brow furrowed as his lips quivered. "My penance was living in a world without her."

"You have got to be kid—"

He threw a branch at me and took off running again. I ducked out of the way and shot after him again, this time hitting him in the shoulder.

He cried out and collapsed to the ground, making a large *thud* against the pile of leaves and brush beneath him.

I ran over to him as he rolled over, his face contorted in pain. I grabbed the front of his robes, lifting him so that his face was inches from mine.

"Did you kill my wife?"

He shook his head, a pained gasp escaping him.

"Did you kill her?"

He shook his head again.

"Answer me, damnit! Did you kill Delphina?"

He sobbed, not even struggling against my grip. "It was an accident. She stumbled into the counter and landed on the floor on top of her knife."

"You pushed her?"

Tears rolled down his gaunt face. He nodded.

Lights flashed off the trees. Running footsteps sounded behind us.

I threw him back onto the ground, and he groaned, rolling to the side to cradle his shoulder.

I stood and waved to the cops coming up, calling out to let them know our location.

As they approached, I looked down at him and felt all the hurt, anger, and grief of the last ten years without Delphina boiling inside me.

I *wanted* to shoot this man.

To kill him right there where he lay. To rid the world of the monster who had taken too many innocent women's lives.

But he had gotten one thing right. Delphina, *my wife*, had been the embodiment of much of what was good and worth safeguarding in this world.

I didn't know what type of woman Delphina would have been now, but I did know she would never go for the kill.

"Kill me." He looked up at me, his greasy hair still in his eyes. "Kill me. It isn't worth living in a world without her. When they take me, there will never be another chance at bringing her back."

I still held my gun, but it was down at my side now. "Believe me, it's *only* because of Delphina that I don't shoot you in the head now," I said. "You're going to prison for a long, long time. You'll be safe there. Might even run into the Limbless Ones again."

He sat bolt upright. "The Limbless—no. No, I can't." He shook his head fast. "Please, just kill me now."

The cops were almost there. I thought I saw the flash of Willow's hair running towards us.

"Please, kill me now!" He rolled himself over to my feet. "I'm begging you!"

"Get off me—"

He grabbed the gun from my hand, put it in his mouth, and fired.

I jumped away from him, falling over on my side. All the figures in my peripheral vision also ducked down.

His body fell backwards with a soft wet rustling of damp leaves.

I stared at it. How had he been strong enough to grab the gun from me? Why hadn't I held it more tightly?

People approached the clearing. Lights were flashed everywhere and urgent voices all merged together.

"Paxton!"

Willow knelt beside me, her hair falling around her face and tickling my nose. The fresh scent of her enveloped me.

I pulled her into a tight embrace, her body half in my lap, right there on the ground in front of everyone.

"Where's Del?" I asked into her hair.

"She's fine. By the time I got her out, Larson and some EMTs took over. I ran out to find you."

I put my forehead to hers. "Are you okay?"

She scoffed, shaking her head as she smiled. "You were almost shot and you're asking if *I'm* okay?" She touched my face, making me look into her eyes. "I'm fine. Are you?"

I pulled her back into me. "I will be."

She and Del were safe, that was all that mattered. I took a deep breath, swallowing the tears threatening to overflow.

Willow. My Willow.

She was real. *She* was here. *She* was in my arms.

"Holt! Grace!"

We looked around, our embrace breaking but we kept our arms around each other.

The Police Chief came running up to us. "Are you guys okay?"

We both nodded.

"That young lady down in the house is getting tended to. She's bruised and in shock, but she'll be okay. She said she's your niece?" I nodded and he looked over at the corpse a few feet away. "That's him?"

We both nodded again.

"I need you to tell me exactly what happened. Larson gave me the best update she could, but—"

"Chief!" a deputy we hadn't met yet ran up to the chief.

"What is it now?" Alvarado threw his hands up.

"You're needed down at the house sir. We found... er, parts in the freezer, sir."

He looked at his deputy in disgust and disbelief. "*Parts?*"

34 WILLOW

I opened my eyes.

The sun shone through a gap in the curtains and alighted on my face. I blinked and rolled over, yawning.

Paxton was laying on the bed beside me, his breathing slow and deep. He was sleeping on his stomach, his arms under his pillow. I admired the muscle definition in his shoulders for a minute before realizing that he wasn't wearing a shirt. Our legs were tangled together, his soft pajama bottoms against the bare skin of my leg.

My cheeks heated before deciding I wasn't going be embarrassed.

I carefully slid out of bed and opened the pass-through door.

Delphi's sleeping form lay on the second bed. I watched for a moment, seeing her chest rise and fall slowly.

It had taken hours for us to leave the crime scene last night, since Delphi hadn't needed to go to the hospital. Her arm and leg sockets were deeply bruised, but other than that, she was unscathed from the whole ordeal. Physically, anyways.

We had to wait for the crime scene to be processed, and an FBI forensic team to come take away Derrick Landon's body which absurdly made me wonder how Solomon and Sinsae were doing. Once all that was completed, Chief Alvarado took Paxton, Delphi and me to the station and asked us to go over everything again, in detail. I relayed everything, starting from when we had left the station after Lox had spilled coffee on me. I made sure to put heavy emphasis on how much help Tony had been to us in solving this case.

The chief told us he would work on Tony getting released, especially since Lox wasn't pressing charges. At that point, both Paxton and Delphi looked like they were going to topple over, they were so tired and emotionally strung out. Both the chief and I had noticed Paxton's arm around Del as she fell asleep on his shoulder. When I'd given the chief a pointed look, he agreed we could leave.

Del had then woken with a start, a look of panic in her eyes.

Paxton had noticed this and said, "It's okay. You're safe. We'll run by your house for you to pick up anything you need and then we'll take you to the motel with us."

When we'd come back to the motel, Paxton packed up his belongings and brought them into my room, giving Delphi his room. He made sure the pass-through door was unlocked for her in case she needed anything before saying goodnight.

Then, without a word, Paxton and I had both undressed, brushed our teeth, and collapsed in my bed. It had been so late that it'd actually been early. We'd passed out before our heads had even hit the pillow.

I closed the pass-through door and heard stirring behind me.

Paxton had propped himself up, now squinting over at me. "Is she okay?" His morning voice sent a shiver through me.

"She seems to be. She's still asleep."

"That's good." His eyes lingered on my bare legs and a small, sleepy smirk formed on his lips. "Did you go to bed wearing such a *scandalous* state of dress?"

"You're one to talk, buddy."

Paxton looked down at his bare chest and his smirk turned a little sheepish. "Touché."

I walked over to the bed and sat against the head board, pulling the blankets over my legs. We both sat in silence for a few minutes and I could feel the sleepy atmosphere turn serious.

"Now what?" We both asked at the same time. Our shared laugh broke the tension.

Paxton sat up and leaned back against the bed frame. "Alvarado seems upset to have missed all the action."

"I mean, he was over-seeing getting that girl's remains to her family."

"True."

I hesitated before asking my next question. "How are you?"

He looked at me, and I watched his eyes unfocus. He reached over and grabbed my hand, gently rubbing his thumb over the back of it. We sat in silence for a few moments as he thought about his answer. Finally, he gave a small shrug. "Muddled."

"I can imagine." I said, putting my other hand over his. "It's been a lot."

"Too much. My brain feels overloaded with all it needs to process."

"I know the feeling."

He looked up at me. "Willow?"

I looked back down at him. "Paxton?"

His eyes traveled between both of mine. With one hand, he intertwined his fingers into mine and with the other, he reached over and ran his hand up my shin.

"Thank you. For being here. I know I've been distant, but you've been there for me through all of this. I know it's your job as my partner, but you've been there for me in more ways than that. This is going to be a long road with me." He took a deep breath. "I know we've been skirting around how official our personal relationship is, and that's kind of my fault. It isn't your job to fix me or bear the weight of my past. But my past is a part of me. And it's clearly something I'm still working through. I never wanted you to see that side of me. And now that you have, I'm kind of relieved. But I also don't want you to feel obligated to stay."

I could feel his hands start to get clammy against my skin. He kept running a finger up and down my shin, but he had stopped looking at me.

I turned my whole body to face him more directly. "As if my past isn't also a burden to bear."

He looked at that. "No, that's not what I—"

"You have seen me in so many instances that were then my worst. You helped me out of jail. You've comforted me when my anxiety is overwhelming. You held me after what happened with Father Flint."

His fingers tightened around mine.

"I am not perfect. I didn't want you to see those sides of me either. But you have and you *stayed*. You fought for me. You have not once left my side. Do you really think I won't do the same for you?"

Tears formed in his eyes and his lower lip began to shake before he clenched his jaw. I ran a finger of my free hand down the side of his face before cupping his cheek. For a long moment we looked at each other.

"I know you will. I trust you. And you know, that's something I don't say to *you* often enough." Then Paxton leaned forward, and I met him in a kiss. I felt my heart rate spike and our kiss deepened.

I wanted him to know how much I meant every word. We were broken individuals, and as much as I wished that he had never endured what he had, there was a part of me that was glad for it. I didn't feel so alone in our partnership anymore, like I was the only one who had a past that made being loved challenging. I didn't feel like he was constantly going to have to be the strong one.

He would need me too. And I wanted to be there for him.

"You know what we need?" Paxton said, breaking apart from me after several long minutes, or possibly a few hours.

"Hmm?" My brain had entirely disconnected. "What is it?"

"We should take a vacation. Just the two of us."

My eyes were still on his lips. "Yeah?"

"Yeah. After we get everything taken care of, we should go."

I smiled at him. "I like the sound of that."

The End

ACKNOWLEDGMENTS

I want to say the biggest thank you to my team at Liquid Mind Publishing.

Thank you, Fiona, for tearing this book apart with your edits and helping me put it back together. You did an amazing job and I can't sing your praises enough. All my love, forever. It wouldn't be what it is now without you.

Thank you, Barb and Blaze, for your incredible work proofing! Your comments and polishing were exactly what this book needed.

Nick, I will be forever grateful for this opportunity you gave me. Thank you all.

Thank you, Brian, for your mentorship and encouragement! I greatly appreciate your taking my emails about dismemberment in stride.

Charlie, your help in solidifying my outline saved my bacon. You're the bestest.

To my family and friends. Your never-ending support, encouragement, and love brought me to where I am today. Thank you, thank you, thank you.

Lastly, to the One above who made all this possible.

ALSO BY WITHOUT WARRANT

More Thriller Series from Without Warrant Authors:

Dana Gray Mysteries by C.J. Cross

Girl Left Behind

Girl on the Hill

Girl in the Grave

Girl Betrayed (Coming Soon!)

The Kenzie Gilmore Series by Biba Pearce

Afterburn

Dead Heat

Heatwave

Burnout

Deep Heat

Fever Pitch

Storm Surge

Night Watch (Coming Soon!)

Willow Grace FBI Thrillers
by Without Warrant and C. C. West

Shadow of Grace

Condition of Grace

Hunt for Grace

Time for Grace

Piece of Grace (Coming Soon!)

Gia Santella Crime Thriller Series
by Kristi Belcamino

Vendetta

Vigilante

Vengeance

Black Widow

Day of the Dead

Border Line

Night Fall

Stone Cold

Cold as Death

Cold Blooded

Dark Shadows

Dark Vengeance

Dark Justice

Deadly Justice

Deadly Lies

Vigilante Crime Series by Kristi Belcamino

Blood & Roses

Blood & Fire

Blood & Bone

Blood & Tears

Queen of Spades Thrillers by Kristi Belcamino

Queen of Spades

The One-Eyed Jack

The Suicide King

The Ace of Clubs

The Joker

The Wild Card

High Stakes

Poker Face

Join Without Warrant's private reader group on Facebook!

ABOUT THE AUTHOR

C. C. West is not used to speaking in third person about herself so I will abruptly cease to, jarring as it is.

Hello there, it's delightful to meet you! When I'm not writing, you can find me hiking, watching some TV show or other, or dancing in my kitchen to Bryan Adams while making cookies. While I currently live on the western side of the USA, I have lived and traveled to many places in my life (which is why I add random 'u's to words like 'colour' and find myself in a perpetual state of high dudgeon over fellow Americans calling that dry triangle pastry a 'scone').

How do you conclude an author bio? I dunno, so I'll end with saying this from the heart: I'm so glad you're here.

instagram.com/c.c.westauthor

tiktok.com/@c.c.westauthor

aa9341fa-96a5-49b2-9e2f-1dd50868d160R01